LIFE
STORY
TERROR

DAVID WISE

The story of three families, through the generations, where revenge played a major part in their lives.

Copyright

All rights reserved. 'Life Story Terror' by David Wise in its current format, copyright © D. Wise 2016. This book in part or in whole, may not be copied or reproduced in its current format by any means, digital, in print or otherwise without written permission, except for quotations for review purposes only.

Tempus Books
The Old Yard
171 Southport Road
Scarisbrick
West Lancs
PR8 5LE
www.tempusbooks.com
email: enquiry@tempusbooks.com

ISBN-13: 978-1530846771
ISBN-10: 1530846773

LIFE STORY TERROR

LIFE STORY TERROR
Cast Of Characters

Joe Wiles—narrator—1938—
Arthur Wiles—Joe's paternal grandfather—1870—1922
Louise Wiles—Joe's paternal grandmother—1874—1964
Louis Wiles—Joe's father—1899—1954
Ann Wiles, nee Mickon—Joe's mother—1903—1960
Sarah Wiles—Joe's wife—1938—1989

Nickolas Mickon—Joe's maternal grandfather—1875—1925
Anna Mickon—Joe's maternal grandmother—1877—1925
Millie Mickon—Joe's aunt—1901—1972

Tom Cradock—The gangster, from Reading, England, who stalked Art Wiles—1870—1923
John Cradock—Tom's son—1900—1956
Jim Cradock—John's son—1934—2007
Ed Cradock—Jim's son—1970—

Janos Kovak—Austrian army agent—1876—1927
Charlie—Joe's King Charles spaniel

CHAPTER ONE

TIMELINE- 2016
There was an antiseptic smell in the room...
A seventy-eight year old man was sitting in a wheelchair by a window, thinking about the life story he had written. He was staring at his reflection in the window. His hair was white and stringy, his long sideburns reached down past his earlobe. His eyes were watery and blue with crow's feet underneath. His face was world weary and wrinkled. His fingers, that gripped the arms of the chair, were gnarled. He smiled at his reflection, but it was a spiritless smile, as if his life and old age had beaten him down. He turned away from the window and looked at the picture of his dog, Charlie, which was on the dresser. In his mind, the dog asked him questions as a prompt for his writing. He smiled again and turned back to the window. Now, he was looking at himself as a young man, thick brown hair combed back in a quiff, bright blue eyes, smooth skin over chiseled features and his

fingers weren't gnarled, they were straight and strong. He looked at the reflection with tears running down his cheeks. His mind returned to his life. As the story unfolded, what terror emerged?

***

"Don't hurt me, please, I'm an old man! Oh, no, it's you!" Charlie started to bark...
TWO YEARS EARLIER:

I love this room, it's my writing room, where my novels were born. I'm surrounded by book shelves filled with fiction and non-fiction books and many items of memorabilia from my life. The walls are covered with the covers of my books, certificates of achievement from various writing courses, and photos of my family and myself.

My name is Joe Wiles, and this is Charlie, by my side, my faithful King Charles Spaniel. He's looking up at me with those soulful eyes of his. I'm telling Charlie the story of my life.

People do talk to their dogs especially when they live alone. So, I have long conversations with Charlie all the time. He understands my body language and the tone of my voice. Talking to Charlie always helps me get difficult issues out in the open and work through emotional discussions such as my life story memories.

I love Charlie and we live as "one being". We have a great interaction together. I get inspiration from Charlie. He gives me so much love and affection, and that makes me happy. When he sees me he dances with excitement. He is always happy to see me.

When I'm feeling down, there is always my pal, Charlie, waiting for a snuggle and it makes me feel better. He loves to listen to the sound of my voice. He's getting old now, just like me, we are getting mellow, frail and grumpy, but we're still old friends.

Charlie is my confidant and now that I'm recalling my life, I'm telling him too. It helps me sort things out as I am writing.

***

I just passed my seventy-sixth birthday so I thought it was time to recall some of my life stories. Maybe, my story and my family's story are important to somebody, maybe, many somebodies! I have a story to pass on to people who knew me and to unknown future generations! I told the publisher of my other novels of my intention to write my life story memories. She said it was a good idea, so I went ahead with it and now it is published.

The story helped me understand my family dynamics, the forces which stimulated change and progress. Someone once told me that when I write my life story, I will feel wiser. I wonder how much wisdom I gained from the preservation of my story. In recalling my story, I hope it will bring understanding about "Who I Am" and "Who They Were". I might learn who I am today from who I was earlier in my life.

"Why did you write your life story?" said Charlie, "I'm curious."

"I knew that the very act of writing would force me to think and rethink about my past and present situations, the people around me, and the events that made my life extraordinary."

"Does this autobio exercise define you?"

"Yes, it does. I hope it shows the world, "I was here and I mattered!" Writing my memories gave me the opportunity to reach across the limits of time and space. It allowed me to tell my side of the story."

"Will your life story help you restore friendly relations between people?"

"I hope so, Charlie, but if it doesn't reconcile the past at least it is good therapy for me. When I tell you the story, you will see the hard times I went through, that left much resentment. I hope some forgiveness will come out of this life story recall."

"So, you want to rid yourself of bad feelings?"

"Yes, I do. In the telling you will see that the Cradock's revenge vendetta against my family triggered bad feelings that festered for years, eroding my happiness and my family's."

"Will you learn something from your life story project?"

Life Story Terror

"Yes, in the recording of events in my life, the tragedies and the dramas, will, I hope, provide insights for me and others that read it."

***

"Well Charlie, what is your first question about my life?"

Charlie, the curious dog, looked up at me.

"What did you say, Charlie?"

I listened intently.

"Oh! What about my grandparents?"

I stroked Charlie's head and said:

"I only knew one of my grandparents, my Dad's mother. She died when I was twenty-one. My mother's parents died in a fire before I was born. But the one I'm really interested in, is my Dad's father, my grandfather, Arthur Wiles. He was the one that came from Reading, England and ended up in Chicago. I always wished I could have met him."

Charlie nudged my leg.

"Why did your grandfather leave his family and travel such a great distance?"

There was silence, I was thinking. Charlie cocked his head and stared at me.

"Well, my Dad, Louis Wiles, told me his father, Arthur, owed some money to a gangster named Tom Cradock. Cradock and my grandfather went to the same school. My grandfather fell in love with Cradock's girlfriend and then she finished with the gangster. He threatened and physically assaulted Arthur. Consequently, my grandfather retaliated by confidentially telling the police about Cradock's activities."

"What happened next?" said the curious dog.

"Jobs in England were not plentiful at the time so my grandfather decided to leave for America, where there were plenty of jobs, some of which were advertised in the news papers. So, Arthur Wiles, left England in 1890, at the age of twenty, and ended up in Chicago, Illinois, USA. But, what he didn't know was that Cradock followed him on the next boat.

Charlie asked: "What was Cradock's background?"

"Well, Charlie, my friend, I'll tell you what my father's journal stated:

Tom Cradock belonged to a gang of hoodlums who robbed people and burglarized businesses in 1888 Reading, England. The streets of Reading were gripped by street warfare. Cradock was a dangerous person even capable of murder!

In England's industrial revolution, the gulf between the rich and poor was marked by slums, where Cradock grew up. My grandfather lived a couple of blocks away in a better area but Tom and Art went to the same school. Because Art owed Tom money and also the fact that Art liked the gangster's girlfriend, there was little love between the two young men.

Life Story Terror

The incident that precipitated the riff to the point of Art leaving Reading for American and Cradock following him, happened when Cradock was on his way to a gang war. My grandfather was walking home when Cradock spotted him.

TIMELINE 1889

"Hey Wiles, I want you to stop sniffing around my girl, understand?"

Now Cradock was a scary figure, with his evil eyes and his hair parted down the middle and pasted down on both sides. He was wearing a black coat and trousers, with a flashy white silk scarf around his neck, the uniform of the hoods. He had his belt in his hand with its heavy buckle, which would be used as a weapon.

"Listen Cradock, it's her choice who she wants to go out with."

With that, Cradock charged my grandfather swinging the buckle end of his thick leather belt above his head. It hit Art Wiles in the head above his eye. It started spurting blood immediately. My grandfather fell to the ground holding his hand over the wound. Cradock ran away.

My grandfather got up and went home holding his hanky on the open wound. He ran past the factories belching out steam and smoke. At home his mother dressed the wound, but a scar remained for the rest of his life.

That was the last straw for Art Wiles. He now was more determined than ever to go to America and seek a better life, but not before he told the police about Cradock."

After my grandfather told the police about Cradock and his gang, they were hot on the heels of the gangster, his family, and his cohorts. Cradock slipped away but his cronies were arrested and his family shamed. Cradock wanted revenge, so he left England for America, following my grandfather.

Arthur Wiles ended up as a buyer for a large department store in Chicago in 1891. Cradock bought a tavern in downtown Chicago where he could continue his gangster ways.

***

CHAPTER TWO

My mind is wandering... I feel a prick in my arm, like something is being injected into me.

I'm hyperventilating. I can't breathe! I'm trying to run away from my body, but I can't move. My heart is beating fast. I feel up one moment and down the next, like a rollercoaster. My vision is blurred. The walls seem to be closing in on me. Panic is setting in. I'm breathing slower now. I want to escape these feelings, but I can't. The walls have eyes, everything around me is staring at me! My body is going numb. Now, it's pins and needles all over!

In the distance I hear Charlie bark, but I feel dizzy... There's a white clad figure near me. It's all a bit dream-like!

TIMELINE—1890

"I guess now we'll find out if the streets are really paved with the gold of opportunity." I heard someone say.

"Where am I?" I asked the fellow ahead of me in line. He turned around and my god, it was my grandfather! He had a tag pinned to his jacket saying, "Arthur Wiles".

The line of people was moving slowly.

"You're in the port of entry hall in America," he said proudly.

I just stood there staring at my grandfather.

"Did you see the Statue of Liberty coming in? It was a wonderful sight. To me it was like one of the seven wonders of the world." My grandfather was beaming.

I must be back in 1890 and all these people here are just off the boat. We were directed through the main doorway and up a steep stairway to a room marked, "Registry". A few people were at the top of the stairs watching us climb the stairs.

"Who are they?"

"Probably, doctors checking for signs of lameness, or heavy breathing that might indicate a heart problem or bewilderment gazes that might mean a mental condition," said my grandfather, knowingly, "It's all a weeding out process."

Next we were in another line and a doctor was checking our faces, hair, neck and hands. Then on to the "eye man", checking for eye diseases that could cause blindness. All these checks were to see if you would be fit for work.

A sign hanging above the exam tables read:

"If immigrants have any of the diseases proscribed by the immigration laws or are too ill or feeble minded to work, they will be deported."

Life Story Terror

After the medical exams, the next line took us through the questioning process. This was designed to verify items of information contained on the manifest.

After our questioning, my grandfather and I were given a nod of approval from the inspector and allowed to pass. My grandfather was going to Chicago, so the next stop for him was the railroad ticket office.

"Well, this is where I leave you," said my grandfather, smiling.

He held out his hand and we both had a good firm handshake. It was great, I had met my grandfather in the flesh!

"What made you come to America?" I had to know.

"Well, living conditions and job prospects weren't good in England after the Industrial Revolution. I read about a buyer's job in Chicago in the newspaper. Also, I got tangled up with a gangster who threatened me, so I decided to leave and have an adventure."

"How was your journey?"

"Not easy! It was frightening really, steerage was very uncomfortable, being in the bowels of the ship. The ventilation was terrible and consequently the air was foul. People were vomiting from seasickness. Most of us stayed in our berths for a large part of the voyage, in a semi-conscious stupor. The food repelled us but we had to eat. We had no washing provisions to keep clean. All this was aggravated by the crowding of bodies together in close quarters. In spite of all that, I have an overwhelming faith in the future. I know things will work out."

Tears of joy were in my grandfather's eyes. Then he disappeared into the railroad ticket office.

I felt drained and then I heard Charlie's bark!

***

I couldn't believe it, I had met my grandfather after his journey across the Atlantic ocean, at the port of entry in N.Y.! It must have been the panic attack that initiated the experience in my mind's eye.

I'm sure the reason I am hallucinating about the past is because of the panic attacks that were plaguing me ever since I started writing my life story. They come in response to various memories of past events. The strange thing is that they seem so REAL.

Even though the sudden surge of physical arousal can be uncomfortable, it does serve a purpose if I can go back in time and meet my family at different points of my life story.

I admit it is very scary going through the physical symptoms and their corresponding thoughts. During the attack I get:

Heart palpitations and immediately I think, "I'm going to have a heart attack!"

Then come the dizzy sensations and I think, "I'm going to pass out!"

My legs get rubbery and I think, "I'm going to fall!"

I usually cope with the attacks by:

Facing the symptoms and not running from them in a frenzy. I say to myself: "I want to find out about my family, so I have to handle the symptoms."

I accept what my body is doing, I just have to float with it.

"This will pass, I'll let my body do its thing and I'll move through it," I think.

But, in the meantime, by jumping into the past and joining my family at different times, supplies me with valuable insights into my life story. When I come back from the past, I always feel a bit "spacey" but I manage to keep control. It's worth it if I can be with my family for a few minutes!

***

A thought suddenly entered my head:

"What about my grandparents on my mom's side?"

I swear Charlie nodded his head!

"According to my mother, her father, Nickolas Mickon, my grandfather, came over to America first, before his wife and baby girl. He was born in 1875 in Austria. He left from Bremen port in Germany and arrived in N.Y. in Feb., 1901.

His wife, Anna, my grandmother, was born in 1877, also in Austria. She left with their baby girl from La Havre, France and arrived in N.Y. in Sept., 1901, seven months after her husband. In that time, he set up house in Port Washington, Wisconsin, where many Slovaks settled."

I felt a prick in my arm again. Oh! Oh! It was happening again! I was starting to hyperventilate. My heart was racing. I felt dizzy…

TIMELINE 1901

"Hold on lady, the sea is rough today," said a voice.

There at the railing on the lower deck of the steamship, stood a young lady, holding a baby tightly in her arms. I walked over and said:

"Lady, are you alright?"

She turned around, and I held my breath, it was my grandmother! She was just like a photo my mother showed me!

"We are a little weak because we have been seasick for the last five days."

The baby was crying.

"This is my daughter, my husband is waiting for us in America." She managed a slight smile.

Just then a large wave hit the ship.

"No, no," she screamed and almost dropped the baby in the ocean.

I gasped in horror as my grandmother managed to hold on to her daughter. I took my grandmother by the hand and led her and the baby to a seat away from the railing. We were slipping and sliding because of the rough sea. The saltwater spray pelted our faces.

"Hold on to the baby," I shouted.

We sat for a bit in silence, trying to get our bearings.

"Why have you and your husband left Europe?"

She rocked her baby and said:

"My husband was in the Austrian army, he wanted to leave but couldn't. You see, the Austrian-Hungarian Empire has forced military service and there is a lot of oppression of the working people, so we thought we'd look for a better life in America."

My grandmother was shivering. I put my arm around her.

"You and your baby better go below now, it's cold up here on deck."

"Thanks for showing us kindness, mister."

My grandmother extended her hand and we shook hands firmly. Then she and her baby disappeared below deck. The baby she almost dropped in the ocean must have been my aunt Millie, my mother's older sister. I was elated that I had met my grandmother, I always wanted to meet her in the flesh.

The story goes that some immigrants from Austria, my maternal grandfather included, were fleeing punishment for emigration to America. They left Austria to avoid the forced military service in the Austrian army.

Sometimes, people were followed all the way to America by agents of the Austrian government to inflict punishment for fleeing conscription.

Janos Kovac, was the man that followed my grandfather on the next boat. His mission was to make my grandfather, Nickolas Mickon's life miserable for avoiding the draft.

I remember what my mother told me about her father being stalked by Kovac. I visualized it in my mind's eye.

TIMELINE 1905

"I'm off to work, Anna," said my grandfather to his wife.

He was walking down the street to the furniture factory when he was accosted by Janos Kovac.

"Get out of my way, I'll be late for work."

Kovac stood his ground.

"Who are you, anyway?"

Kovac smiled an evil smile.

"I'm Janos Kovac, agent for the Austrian army."

"What do you want?"

"I'm here to punish you for leaving the army when you knew it was mandatory to stay."

"I'm in America now, you don't have any rights here," said my grandfather, trying to push past the burly agent.

"There is nothing stopping me from making your life and the lives of your family miserable."

With that, Kovac pushed Nickolas and he fell hard to the ground.

Kovac laughed and said:

"Don't relax for a minute, Mickon, because I will be back."

My grandfather got up and limped to work. He had hurt his leg falling to the ground. He thought to himself:

"With the hardship of working in the factory, now he had to endure the menace of Kovac. The hours at the factory were long, ten hours per day, six days per week. He only made $6 per week to support his family. He worked on a wood turning machine in a small enclosed area and the fumes would make him sick at the end of the day."

That day, he turned up fifteen minutes late and lost an hour's pay! Kovac had started his punishment. There was much worse to come!

TIMELINE 1898, CHICAGO

Tom Cradock married a south side Irish woman and they had one son, John. My paternal grandfather, Art Wiles, married in 1898 to a religious woman, Louise. She gave birth to my father, Louis, in 1899.

Cradock started stalking my grandfather as soon as he located him in Chicago. He was a good detective as well as a gangster! The first time Art Wiles saw Tom Cradock staring at him from across the street, he had a panic attack. These attacks were to run in the family from my grandfather, to my father, to me, because of the Cradock's terrorization of the Wiles family.

"What did you say Charlie?" I stroked his head.

"Oh, you want to know exactly what is stalking?'

I pondered that question for a moment.

"Well, stalking consists of constant attempts to gain control over someone and terrorize them. These people pop up when you least expect it, watching, always watching. The stalker causes emotional terror to their victim.

In the case of Tom Cradock, he wanted revenge on my grandfather for getting the police onto him and his gang. He wanted to disrupt Art's life.

Arthur changed his routine constantly but Cradock always seemed to turn up. It was extremely annoying to be watched and followed many times a month."

My grandfather never told his wife or my father how he was being terrorized by Cradock. He just recorded everything in his journal which he passed on to my dad right before he died.

***

CHAPTER THREE

My grandfather, Arthur Wiles, died in 1922 of TB, but he was made a nervous wreck by Cradock's continuous stalking. Tom Cradock died a year after my grandfather. It was as though his terror work was done. He left his tavern and his hatred to his son, John. So now, my father, Louis, had John Cradock to deal with. They both were in their early twenties.

My Dad, Louis, had an unsettling childhood. His parents, being religious, wanted him to become a lay minister in the protestant religion. They pushed my father into studying religion and also into grueling piano lessons playing classical music and religious hymns. These two pursuits occupied my father from five to fifteen years old. He rebelled in his adolescence against all of this. He did go to college for a while, but didn't follow it up.

TIMELINE 1923-1935

By 1923 my father was a disillusioned young man caught between prohibition and the prospect of supporting his mother on meager wages. He thought the world was against him. And on top of everything, there was John Cradock popping up. He was running his tavern as a speakeasy with a candy store in front as a disguise.

Then along came the 1929 stock market crash and the Great Depression. Now, there were hardly any jobs available. The only good thing that happened around that time was in 1933 prohibition was repealed, so people could drink legally again.

John Cradock got married and they had a son named Jim. Cradock made the tavern into a showcase watering hole with the money he made selling illegal booze. He continued stalking my father.

Jobs were so hard to get, that once my Dad hitch hiked to N.Y. on a freight train box car to get a job as a typist. The job lasted six months, so he came back to Chicago.

My father wrote a journal, which was passed down to me. That's how I know all this information.

***

In April of 1935, my father went to "John Cradock's Piano Bar", located near the main post office just west of downtown Chicago. He was going to have it out with Cradock about the stalking business. It was getting on my father's nerves, just as it did with my grandfather.

It was the height of the Great Depression. According to my Dad's journal, he felt like the world was a disaster, it was falling apart. There had been very hard times for the five years since the Stock Market crash. My father could only find part time work. Unemployment was running at 25% in the city!

The streets were very depressing, people sleeping in doorways, soup kitchens and bread lines, where you could get a bowl of soup and a slice of bread free. But that was the extent of the assistance.

Franklin D. Roosevelt, the 32nd president, was slowly bringing back some optimism with his New Deal program of make-work projects, like the W.P.A., the Works Progress Administration. This provided work for the unemployed, to preserve their skills and self-respect. Road and housing construction and park projects were created.

It was good the New Deal started because people's dignity was at rock bottom! Vagrancy and stealing were frequent charges in arrest and detention. But what could you expect, people had to survive anyway they could. Clothes disappeared off of wash lines, milk from porches. These were desperate times, there were no jobs, and not much government help, so people became petty criminals!

***

I was feeling dizzy again and my breathing was quickening...
　TIMELINE 1935
　　"Buy an apple, mister?"

I looked around and there was a woman, shabbily dressed, selling apples out of a wooden crate.

"They're only a nickel apiece."

I gave her a nickel but I didn't take the apple. I walked a few more yards down the street and found myself in front of "Cradock's Piano Bar", as the neon sign flickered. Across the street I saw about thirty disillusioned men standing in a line. I stopped a passer-by and asked:

"What are those men waiting for?"

"Haven't you seen a bread line before, mister? Those fellas finally plucked up the courage, even though they feel shame, to stand and be seen publicly in a bread line for free food."

I shook my head and walked into "Cradock's Piano Bar". This was the tavern where my father met my mother.

When my eyes adjusted to the dim lighting, I took a look around. There was a large "Stars and Stripes" flag draped on the ceiling over the long bar. Twenty stools were lined up in front of the bar and five tables and chairs opposite the bar. A large stuffed moose head hung on one wall and a photo of FDR on the other. In a corner was an old upright piano. A chubby lady with henna rinsed hair, wearing a black net dress with a large white carnation, was playing tunes and singing.

Behind the bar was a mirror as long as the bar with liquor bottles lined up on either side of a large cash register. Four beer taps with brand markers were all shined up.

There were a couple of men with glasses of beer in front of them, staring at themselves in the mirror. I took a stool at the end of the bar. The barkeep came over and said:

"What'll ya have, buddy?" He had a monogram on his white shirt, JC.

"I'll have a bottle of beer, please."

This guy must be John Cradock, the son of Tom Cradock, who followed my grandfather to America. He was heavy set, about six feet tall with brown hair and large deep set eyes, a wide mouth and a stubble of beard.

"Here ya go, mister. That'll be a quarter."

I gave him the twenty-five cents and poured my beer into a glass. The chubby lady was playing and singing: "Happy Days Are Here Again". FDR's democratic party's theme song in 1932 and 1933. Prohibition was repealed, so it was "happy days".

The door opened and in walked a man with a worn suit and fedora. He sat on the next stool to me. It was my father at thirty-five years old!

"What do you want, Wiles?" said Cradock in an unfriendly way.

"Glass of beer."

Cradock brought the beer and surprisingly he had a smile on his face. My father slid a dime over the bar.

"Cradock, I want you to stop following me, it's getting on my nerves."

Cradock's face softened and he said:

"I have stopped! I'm as tired of it as you are and I'm sorry I've worked you up so much."

"Well, I'm glad to hear that. This stalking has been going on ever since our fathers came from England, it's about time it stopped."

Cradock went to serve someone else on the other end of the bar.

"I couldn't help but hear you two," I said, "It seems you have worked out your disagreement."

My Dad looked at me and smiled, "Yes, so it seems, but I still don't trust him!"

Chubby continued singing, "Happy Days Are Here Again", in a loud voice.

The door of the tavern opened and in walked a tall, slim woman wearing white slacks, a dark top and a short black jacket. She was good looking, with smiling eyes, brown hair with a flower in it slanted to one side. It was my mother at thirty-three years old! She sat on the stool next to my father and ordered a glass of beer.

"Hello, haven't seen you in here before," said my Dad, smiling.

"This is my first time here."

Chubby started playing and singing:

"Red sails in the sunset, way out on the sea..."

My mother started to sing along. When the song finished everyone in the bar clapped, all except

Cradock. He was watching my father and mother intently. I think I was the only one that noticed Cradock's indifference.

"That was wonderful singing, what's your name?" said my dad.

"Ann, what's yours?"

"Lou, Lou Wiles. I really enjoyed your singing, Ann."

"Thank you, Lou."

"Are you from Chicago, Ann?"

"No, I'm from Racine, Wisconsin, but I was born and bred in Port Washington, Wisconsin."

"How about you, Lou?"

"Born and bred in Chicago. Things were better here before the Depression, but now times are hard."

"Yes, I know," my mother said with a serious look on her face.

My dad shook his head and said:

"I've been existing on sinkers and coffee."

"Sinkers?"

"They're doughnuts," laughed my dad.

Chubby started up again, this time it was, "Smoke Gets In Your Eyes". My mother sang the whole song along with Chubby.

"During this gloomy Depression, I find solace in classical music and pop songs," said my dad

"So do I, Lou, I love singing."

"I play the piano a little and I find music helps me deal with loneliness and sadness in these hard times."

"I've been very lonely and sad these past few years," said my mother with tears in her eyes.

"What happened?"

"You don't want to hear about my troubles, Lou."

"Nonsense, it helps to talk about it," said my dad.

"Well, my sister, Millie, lives in Chicago, but we don't get along and I've had some very traumatic experiences back in Wisconsin...," my mother hesitated.

"Keep going, Ann, I'm a good listener. Trust me, it is better to get it out of your system."

"My parents were followed to America from Europe by an agent of the Austrian army. He was to inflict punishment on my father for leaving the army.

For several years he stalked my parents making their life miserable. Then he did the most terrible deed.

TIMELINE 1926

I was twenty-three years old. I was walking home from work and thinking what a beautiful sleepy town Port Washington was, nestled on the coast of Lake Michigan. As I approached the street where I lived, I saw billowing black smoke rising up to the sky. I started running, and then I saw it was my parent's home on fire. I screamed:

"Oh no, my parents are in there, help!"

A fireman came and restrained me from running into the flaming house. I heard another fireman say, it was purposely set with kerosene. I was crying so much I could hardly comprehend what I was witnessing. The firefighters couldn't get close enough to rush into the house, it was an inferno fuelled by the kerosene that I knew Janos Kovac had poured around the doors and windows. In the end, the fire devoured everything in its path leaving only charred remains and black smoke.

Now, my sister and I were orphans. I thought, how could Kovac do such a thing just because my father left the army for America. Kovac disappeared for a while but he popped up again after one year."

"What a tragedy, Ann," said my dad, shaking his head.

My mother continued:

TIMELINE 1927

"A year later Kovac appeared again. I was coming home from work and a car sped up to the curb and stopped."

"Hey, Ann Mickon, I want to talk to you," said Kovac, as he got out of the car and pulled a knife.

I started to run, but he caught me and forced me into the car at knife point. He jumped in and we sped off.

"I'm not finished exacting punishment on the Mickon family," he snarled.

He drove out to the countryside. Fear took hold of me and gave me a burst of adrenalin. I grabbed the steering wheel and tried to step on the brake pedal.

"Get off the wheel, you crazy woman, you'll kill us both."

The car sped around a bend and then crashed through a guard rail and fell fifteen feet into a ravine. We hit a tree and the front end of the car crumpled. My head hit the windscreen. I looked over at Kovac, he was slumped over the steering wheel which was pushed into his chest. There was a trickle of blood coming from a wound on my forehead. I knew I was lucky to be alive.

I tried the car door, but it was jammed. Then I smelled smoke. The car was filling with fumes. My eyes began to water and my throat was burning. I knew if I didn't get out of that car, the smoke would kill me. Then the engine caught fire and I saw flames appear between the twisted metal. I frantically pound on the jammed door. The door finally swung open and I fell out on the ground.

I was very weak and I knew I was in danger of passing out. I could feel the heat from the engine. If the fire got to the petrol tank the explosion would snuff out my life. With superhuman strength I got up and staggered away from the burning car. I must have gotten about fifteen yards away when the car exploded. I was thrown to the ground and landed on my arm. The car was sending black smoke into the air.

My arm was hurting and it was bent at a strange angle but I was alive!

"Lady, can you hear me?" was the last thing I heard before I passed out. I woke up in the hospital with a broken arm but that was the end of Janos Kovac!"

My dad put his arm around my mother. You could see she was very shaken by her explanation of the traumatic events.

We all ordered another round of beers. Chubby was playing, "Happy Days Are Here Again", for the third time.

We were all silent for a few minutes. Then my dad broke in and said:

"I find loneliness is a dark place where you are waiting for someone to come and put the light on."

"That's very profound, Lou," said my mother.

"When two lonely people meet that means their loneliness is doubled," continued my father.

"But Lou, when the light goes on, their joy is also multiplied."

We all joined in with Chubby to sing a chorus of "Happy Days"!

"Lets get out of here and go for a walk, Ann."

"Okay Lou, I could use some fresh air."

Before they left, I shook hands with them both and wished them well. It was great, I had been there when my folks met!

I sat there alone finishing up my beer and observing John Cradock. The way he talked to his customers was patronizing. No matter how he tried to smooth it over with my dad, he still impressed me as a nasty piece of work.

***

I was breathing slower now and I heard a sharp bark from Charlie.

"Boy oh boy, Charlie, this life story stuff is like peeling away the layers of an onion!"

CHAPTER FOUR

It was April, 1939, the date on the photo. My mother was sitting on a park bench on Buena Avenue with me, at nine months old, with casts on both legs and feetI often wondered how my mother coped in those early days. I was sitting on my mother's lap as a baby, in the photo I had a distressed look on my face. The casts were clearly very uncomfortable.

I closed my eyes, trying to calm the panic that I felt rising...

TIMELINE 1939

"Hello, may I sit down?"

"Sure you can," said my mother, smiling.

"That's a cute baby. What's his name?"

"Joe."

"Hello Joe," he didn't smile, just kept looking at the casts.

"Why has he have casts?"

My mother winced.

"Joe was born with clubfeet."

"Oh, I'm so sorry."

"He's doing fine, we're getting the best treatment."

"What hospital are you with?"

"Joe is a charity case at Billings Hospital on the far south side. He spent the first six months of his life in hospital."

Just then, I noticed a man watching us from the shadows across the street.

"Do you know that man over there?" I pointed across the street.

"I don't think so, but I've seen him a few times around here. It's scary, but he always stays across the street. He probably doesn't mean any harm.'

I recognized him. It was John Cradock from the Piano Bar. My mother probably forgot the bartender at the tavern where she met my dad. When I looked again he had disappeared!

"How are you coping with little Joe?" I asked.

"It's hard at times but I focus so much on Joe that it takes away some of the stress."

"Do you have a husband to help you?"

"Yes, but he doesn't live with me here. He's with his mother and sister, helping them with their bills. His family don't know about Joe yet. He just got a part time job at the main post office in Chicago."

"That doesn't sound like an ideal situation."

"He comes to visit Joe and I almost every day."

My mother had a far away look in her eyes.

"I get lonely sometimes but Joe keeps me busy. We have to go to the hospital quite often."

Life Story Terror

"It must be tough on you and little Joe. Sometimes having children with afflictions compounds stress."

My mother nodded her head.

"Sometimes I get so tired, I don't even take a shower. When I get Joe to sleep, I just fall asleep with him!"

Little Joe started to cry. My mother started rocking him.

"The casts bother him," she whispered.

We were silent for a minute and I noticed Cradock was nowhere to be seen. I wondered how much of a danger he was. That thought made me nervous.

"I've had to go through a lot of adjustment because it is very traumatizing having a child with a disability."

My mother started to ramble on, but it was probably good for her to get things off her chest.

"What kind of adjustment?"

"Well, I had difficulty accepting Joe's affliction. I kept asking, "Why Joe? Why me?""

"It's hard to answer some "Why" questions. Life is unfair but we must try to do the best we can in all situations."

"I went through a stage of anger. Finally, I became resigned to the fact that Joe had a disability, which we had to deal with. When I accepted that fact, I was so glad he was getting good care."

"You seem to be coping now," I smiled.

"Yes, now I am, I understand and appreciate Joe and I am trying to strengthen myself so I will be able to help Joe through this."

Little Joe was fast asleep.

"Yes, I'm doing okay now. I can talk about Joe's affliction without rage."

We both smiled at each other.

"Well, I better get home and put Joe in his cot, nice talking to you mister."

"Talking helps sometimes."

"Yes, it sure does."

"Well, good luck to you and little Joe," I said as we shook hands.

My mother and Joe disappeared into the adjacent apartment building. I felt good that I might have eased my mother's anxiety a little.

Charlie was licking my hand.

"It's okay, Charlie, I'm back."

***

"Tell us about the time Cradock ruined a nice day in the park for you and your parents."

"Okay Charlie, I remember that day vividly."

TIMELINE 1945

The summer air filled Lincoln Park that Sunday. My mother, father and I went there for the day with our packed sandwiches. We were a happy threesome enjoying family life under the blazing sun. We spread our blanket on the lush grass and sat down.

"Oh, look, the ice cream van," I said, pointing in the distance.

My dad went to get three ice cream cones. By the time he got back they were starting to melt, but that was all part of the fun of a day in the park.

Small children were playing, some were crying as their mothers were trying to explain they didn't have any money for ice cream. There were the usual runners dashing around. Some older boys were playing rough house football. We were tucking into our sandwiches and watching the football carnage, full of grazed knees and cries of pain!

There was an old couple walking on the path bearing heavily on their canes. Their aged faces crinkling into smiles as they watched the boys knocking each other over. My mother folded up the blanket and off we went.

"Lets go over to the lagoon and take a ride on a boat," I said, hoping for an "okay" answer.

"Okay," said my parents in unison.

I remember walking between my mom and dad and we all were laughing, it was a good day, so far!

"I know now, what the most precious thing on earth is," said my mother, beaming with happiness.

"What's that?" said my dad.

"It's just being alive, sweetheart! We must live life to the full and not waste a minute of it."

We arrived at the lagoon and there was a rowboat waiting for us. My dad paid for an hour out on the water. We all piled into the aged dingy, my dad grabbed the oars and off we went knocking the floating lily pads out of the way.

We were in the middle of the lagoon, where it was about fifteen feet deep, when we noticed the boat taking on water fast! My mother screamed and I sat there getting my feet wet.

"Hold on, I'm going to row as fast as I can back to shore."

It was a race against the leak in the boat. My dad rowed with all of his strength. We made it about six feet from shore when the boat sank in three feet of water. We waded ashore. The boat tender was full of apologies and he refunded our rental money.

"We could have drowned if the boat went down in deep water," cried my mom.

None of us were very good swimmers.

Just then my dad noticed John Cradock watching us in the distance. He was laughing. Then he disappeared into the crowd.

"He had something to do with the leaky boat," said my dad.

We sat in the sun to dry off and went home sober faced!

***

TIMELINE 1948

My mother didn't go to see her sister, Millie, very often, but when she did, she took me along. I always wondered why my aunt Millie used to say hateful things to my mother all the time.

I remember one such time, I guess I was about ten years old. We took the long ride on public transportation to the south side of Chicago, where Millie and her husband, Frank, lived.

My aunt and uncle scared me because they were so different from my mother. Millie and her husband were old time Slovac types. They liked beer and sausage and didn't keep a very tidy house.

Frank always wanted a son but Millie didn't give him one, so he used to pick me up and ruffle my hair. I remember he always smelled of beer, sausage and strong cheese.

"Anna, you have a good life now, don't you?" said Millie.

She always called my mother, Anna, because she knew my mother preferred to be called, "Ann".

"No thanks to you, Millie. You left me to take care of ma and pa when you got married and moved to Chicago."

"Awah, quit your beefing, I was always good to you, listening to your troubles."

"You mean like the time I was relaxing in a chair with my head back and my eyes closed and you snuck up on me and hit me on the Adam's Apple. I could have died!'

"But you didn't," laughed Millie.

My mother's face was turning red with anger.

"Sometimes I wish mother did drop you in the ocean when she came to
America."

It was quiet except for Millie's husband, Frank, chewing his sausage and drinking his beer.

"Hey, little Joe, do you want to try some of my beer?" said Frank.

I backed away.

"Don't you dare give Joe any beer, he's only ten years old," said my mother, pushing the glass away.

After about an hour of bickering back and forth, my mother said:

"Come on Joe, we're going home, I can't stand to be in this house any longer."

"You'll be back, when you want a shoulder to cry on," said Millie, smirking, "You always thought you were better than me."

When we were walking toward the bus stop, who should pop up but John Cradock.

"Did you have a nice time with your sister?" he said, sarcastically.

My mother brushed by him. I looked back and saw he was knocking on Millie's door. I always wondered if he was making Millie's life miserable also. My mother was a Wiles, by marriage, and Millie was her sister. It would be ironic, if it was true, because then Cradock would be continuing Janos Kovac's punishment!

***

Life Story Terror

TIMELINE 1950

Cradock was still stalking my dad, but now, he was doing something even worse! My father, now, had a full-time job at the post office, but it was on the night shift. He started stopping off after work for a drink.

I was twelve years old and feeling bad about my folks arguing over my dad's drinking. He drank after work at Cradock's Bar. Cradock egged my father on to drink and kept serving him until he was drunk.

When my dad came home at three in the morning, full of drink, that's when I woke up to my mom and dad arguing. It was awful!

I had to find out what was happening and maybe do something about it, but what?

I was getting dizzy again and my arm was aching. I was in a fog and there were people in white clothes running around and then...

I found myself standing outside of Cradock's Bar, the "piano" name was gone. The peculiar thing was, that I wasn't a twelve year old boy but a man about twenty-five!

It was 12:30 AM, the night shift at the post office got off at midnight. I walked through the squeaky door, the mustiness of the tavern hit me. It was run down since the days my parents met there. The piano was no longer in the corner. I looked around and sure enough there was my dad sitting at the end of the bar. He had a glass of beer and a shot glass in front of him, which Cradock was filling up. I sat on the stool next to my dad and ordered a glass of beer.

"It's good to have a beer to unwind after work," I said, smiling at my father.

My dad turned and looked at me with glassy eyes.

"That's what I do all the time is unwind here after work," he slurred.

"Why do you drink so much," I ventured.

"I'm fifty-one years old and my life has been meaningless."

My father swallowed the whiskey shot in one gulp!

"How's that?"

"I studied classical piano and became fairly good at it. I played well, so people told me. I went to college for two years and dropped out. I never held a job that meant anything. I should have amounted to something, but I'm a failure."

Cradock refilled my dad's shot glass. I glared at him, but he just smirked.

"You have a family don't you?"

"Yes, but I've failed at being a husband and father too."

My dad lit up a cigarette and puffed heavily on it.

"And now, I've ended up in this run-of-the-mill night job at the post office. I'm so disappointed in myself."

Life Story Terror

My dad was rambling on about his tough times. This was the first stage of drunkenness, being verbose, talking incessantly.

Then my father put his arm around my shoulders and said:

"You're my friend, aren't you?"

"Yes, of course I am," I replied.

This was the second stage, amicose, everyone is a friend.

My dad then slammed his fist on the bar.

"That bastard barkeep is the problem."

This was the third stage, bellicose, aggressive and ready to fight.

At every stage, Cradock poured my dad another shot. It was heart wrenching to watch my father lose his dignity.

"I don't know what to do," said my father and then he mumbled some swear words.

This was the fourth stage, morose, sullen and bad-tempered.

My dad started crying, tears streaming down his cheeks. I handed him my hanky.

This was the fifth stage, lachrymose, the weepy stage.

My father then started stammering, I couldn't understand a word he was saying.

This was the sixth stage, stuporous, being incoherent.

Finally his head slumped and silence.

This was the final stage, comatose.

With that, my dad laid his head in his arms on the bar, the cig dropped to the floor. I bent down and picked it up and stubbed it out. I noticed there was no money on the bar, apparently Cradock was putting the drinks on a bill. I motioned Cradock over.

"What do you want, mister, another beer?"

"No thanks. I want to ask you a question. Why do you keep feeding this man drinks when you can see he's had enough?"

"Hey, hold on mister, I'm not his keeper and what business is it of yours anyway?"

"I noticed you keep putting his drinks on a tab, how do you think he can pay for all these drinks?"

"He pays when he gets paid."

"Oh, that's great, then his family suffers because he hasn't enough money left to cover the bills."

"Like I said, mister, I'm not his keeper." Cradock laughed wickedly.

"Don't you know that with a liquor license comes responsibility? When you see a person has had enough to drink, you don't serve them anymore."

"What are you, my conscience?"

"I don't think you have one," I said firmly.

"You know mister, you're getting on my nerves," he said, clenching his fist.

I continued, "It's illegal to sell alcohol to someone who is drunk. They could stumble out of here and hurt themselves."

I looked sadly at my dad with his head on the bar. He certainly wasn't happy with his life. The next thing I knew, Cradock had me by the collar and was pushing me out of the tavern.

I opened my eyes feeling groggy and Charlie was staring at me. Now, I knew Cradock was starting a new tactic to ruin my dad and he was capable of any skullduggery!

***

Charlie was whimpering.

"What's the matter, boy?"

He wanted to know about the scary time when I was abducted for a little while by John Cradock.

My mind went back to the past…

TIMELINE 1951

I was thirteen years old and feeling the terrible effects of having a father that was being driven to drink by a revengeful man. I was walking home and my mind was a semi-blank, observing the cars whizzing down the street. Suddenly, a large hand grabbed my shoulder and jolted me back to the present. I turned around and stared at a big man, who had me by the collar of my coat.

"What are you doing?" I stammered.

"Come with me, kid."

And with that, he pushed me into an adjacent alleyway. I struggled in his grasp but to no avail, his grip on my shoulder was vise-like.

"What do you want?" I said, feeling terror streaming through my body.

"Do you know who I am?"

"No, I don't."

"I'm John Cradock, the man who is diminishing your father to a sniveling drunk."

I struggled to get away but he held me tighter and started to shake me violently. My eyes were open wide in terror as he said:

"Now, you listen to me kid. I want you to tell your dad that when I'm finished with him, I'm going to start on you!"

He shoved me so hard that I fell backwards to the ground. Cradock came toward me menacingly, but I yelled, "Get away from me."

Cradock stopped advancing toward me and he started laughing uncontrollably. I scrambled to my feet and ran away. When I looked back Cradock was gone! I didn't tell my parents about the incident, they had enough problems and anyway there was nothing anybody could do.

The memory quickly vanished and only Charlie was with me.

***

CHAPTER FIVE

TIMELINE 1954

When I went to my dad's funeral I was fifteen years old. I was shocked that my father had been run down by a car because he was too drunk to cross the street properly. He had been drinking after work for years at Cradock's tavern. John Cradock had always encouraged my dad to drink more and more, knowing this would eventually ruin his family life. Cradock had exacted his family's revenge on my family to the nth degree!

I felt abandoned by the loss of my father. I needed my dad more than ever at fifteen. I lost the person that should have been my life guide, answering my questions about the human condition.

This was the event that changed my scope on life completely. Everything about that day and the following weeks was depressing. I was on my own that day at the funeral, without my mother. She couldn't attend because she had a nervous breakdown a couple of years before and now she was a recluse, not going out of the apartment.

I remember when I was about twenty years old, my mother and I had a discussion about my dad's drinking. I started out by saying:

"We knew it was Cradock that was pushing my dad to drink, but why was he able to be pushed? There had to be an underlying cause."

"I think it was depression," said my mom.

"What was he depressed about?"

"Two things, Cradock's revenge vendetta, but mostly about not amounting to much in life."

I shook my head.

"So, I would guess dad's drinking just made his depression worse."

"That's right son, when your dad was drunk he could forget himself."

My mother started crying and stammered:

"I remember those times vividly. I was at my wits end."

I put my arm around my mother.

"When dad was drunk he could refuse to take responsibility for anything. When he was sober it was difficult to deal with his problems," I said sadly.

"I used to argue with your father but it didn't do any good and I was always afraid he'd get violent."

"Sometimes I thought it would be best to remain neutral. But when he came home in a drunken mood I just saw red and raised my voice against him" I was getting choked up now.

"I think your father felt guilty about his weak will but he couldn't help himself."

I held my mom's hand and said:

"All I know is the emotional abuse dad heaped on us had a lasting effect on me. And Cradock took advantage of the situation and encouraged dad to drink futher."

The memory of the discussion started to fade.

Getting back to the funeral...

Oh no! I'm starting to feel dizzy, another panic attack was coming on. In the foggy distance I saw a white coated figure...

I found myself standing outside the funeral parlor. I noticed John Cradock watching from across the street. I went into the death parlor.

"Joe, are you alright?"

It was my grandmother, who I hadn't seen for two years.

"I'm okay," I said sullenly.

The air was musty and there was a hint of cleaner as if to disguise the smell of death! I glanced around, the only other people in the room were my grandmother and the funeral director.

My grandmother looked at me with hatred in her eyes, at least that's the way I saw it. She blamed my mother and I for my dad's drinking, because he didn't have any family life. But that was his fault plus she knew nothing of the Cradock revenge vendetta. My grandfather didn't tell his wife about Cradock but he recorded everything in his journal which he passed on to my dad.

The funeral director led me to a chair in front. Two candles on wooden pillars were burning on each side of the casket. A few flower arrangements were scattered around. But all of that didn't mean anything to me.

I got up and walked slowly to my father's casket. His face was ashen and his head was shaven because they had operated on his head, trying to stop the bleeding inside his brain. There was a white shroud barely covering his now bald head. I just stood there staring, my shoulders slumped under the weight of Death!

I turned around and went back to my seat. The pastor gave a short talk, which I didn't listen to, my thoughts were racing around in my head. I just wanted this gloomy occasion to end.

I told myself, "I won't cry", and I didn't. I glanced at my dad's profile in the casket. This was it; this was the last time I would ever see my dad again! Oh, the finality of it all! There were so many things I wished we could have talked about. My mother and I choose cremation because it was the cheaper option and we were hard up for money.

When I came out of the funeral parlor, I noticed Cradock was still across the street watching. When he saw me, there was a hint of a smile on his face. It was wicked of him and it made my flesh crawl! The funeral director drove me home. I slammed the car door and walked into our apartment building. I told my mom about the day's proceedings, as she cried.

After that, my perspective on life shifted. This was the time when I lost what faith I had. I became an atheist. Death was just a return to nothingness where we all came from. There was no such thing as an afterlife. Death was an end to my father's life, but it affected me for many years. This is the time when I "grew up" and began to understand the significance of life while we have it.

I came back to the present feeling something warm on my hand. It was Charlie licking my fingers.

"Yes Charlie, I'm back."

Charlie looked at me as if he understood what I had been through.

***

TIMELINE 1956

Charlie asked, "What was one of the loneliest days in your life?"

The more I thought about this question, the more I remembered the day of my June, 1956, high school graduation.

John Cradock died in January of 1956 of a heart attack. But it wasn't the end of the Cradocks, his son Jim, took over the stalking duties, he was twenty-three years old and now the owner of Cradock's Bar.

But getting back to my graduation day. It was a warm, muggy day in late June.

"Mom, I'm going now."

My mother gave me a peck on the cheek and wished me well. She was sad, and so was I, that she couldn't go, but the remnants of the breakdown still kept her indoors. I had four tickets to my graduation for my family but I wouldn't need them. Nobody was going to be there for me!

I went into the school building and went directly to the assembly point outside the Auditorium. All my classmates were milling around, putting on their gowns and caps. I went over and put mine on.

"Joe, aren't you excited, we're finally finished?"

"Yes, it's great," I lied.

Another student said, "My dreams of the future can come true, as long as I have the guts to go after them."

I gave him a weak smile.

Another kid came up to me and said:

"When I get my diploma the world will be unlocked to me, it's a passport to freedom."

I nodded and got into the procession line.

"Big day today, Joe, I'm so excited with my family here."

"Yea, a big day," I said soberly.

Everyone wanted their graduation to be a special, memorable occasion, so did I, but it wasn't to be. I just wanted to get it over with. I wanted to get my diploma so I could get a decent job.

The procession music started and I marched into the Auditorium with the other one hundred plus students. I looked straight ahead, knowing no one was there for me. I took my seat.

When the speeches were over, I marched up onto the stage and received my diploma. I then wanted to disappear as fast as possible. I dumped my cap and gown on the table in the hallway and while everyone was talking to their families, I headed for the door, never to enter the building again.

Outside, I took a deep breath of air and hurried down the steps and across the street to go home. Then, Jim Cradock appeared around a corner and said:

"Did you have a nice day, Wiles?"

Cradock was the last person I wanted to see that day. I tried to get past him but he blocked my way.

"Did you have your family there?" he laughed.

I brushed past him, almost tripping, without answering his questions. But I was so angry, I turned around and went right up to him, nose to nose!

"I want you to stop following me. This has gone on far too long between our families. You bug me!"

I don't care whether I bug you or not. What I want to do is upset your life," he smirked.

I poked him in the chest with my finger very hard and said:

"Don't you realize revenge is useless?"

Cradock gave me a push and I went back one step.

"Your grandfather got my family, back in England, into trouble and some were locked up! He was a stoolie!"

"That was in the distant past. My grandfather was probably justified in what he did. You must understand that his harassment won't resolve anything."

"The Cradocks had to retaliate and now I'm here to make your life miserable."

"You still don't get it. You're sustaining your anger over years. The fire inside you is burning your insides and this doesn't do anybody any good."

Cradock gave me another push and I almost fell down.

"I'm not going to fight you. You will see sense in the future, I hope."

"If someone hurts your family, you try to scar them physically and mentally."

Cradock was glaring at me in a murderous way.

"You're still not hearing me, Cradock."

"I hear you, but I feel better when I see you squirm."

"You maybe hearing me, but you're not understanding what I'm trying to get over to you."

Cradock started laughing and he looked the other way trying to ignore me.

"Look at me when I'm talking to you. I tell you this revenge idea of yours will destroy you."

"I don't have to look at you because I don't buy what you're saying. I'm going forward with what my grandfather and father started. What your grandfather did wronged my family and I'm going to be cruel to you no matter what the consequences."

"Cradock you're talking rubbish. You're just saying whatever crap comes into your head to throw me off. But I will not feel guilty about what my grandfather did."

"Do you even realize why after all these years you are seeking revenge?"

"Yes, I do know why I want revenge. Because when I cause you misery, I feel a sense of catharsis. I feel a releasing of repressed emotions and I feel relieved of the burden of carrying them."

I shook my head.

"You still don't understand. When you take revenge you think about it constantly so, instead of providing closure, you're doing the opposite. You're keeping the wound open and fresh!"

"All I can say to you, Wiles, is watch your back because I'll always be close!"

With that he pushed past me and walked away laughing. I went home clutching my diploma. This was the end of a terrible day for me, which was supposed to be happy!

***

TIMELINE 1960

Four years after my high school graduation, my mother died from complications of diabetes. It was a tough time for me, I was twenty-two years old and just getting used to the work-a-day world. I had to organize the funeral and in the end, there was no one there for my mother but me. I buried her in Graceland Cemetery where my dad's ashes were buried. I did see Cradock in the distance at the cemetery which was disconcerting to say the least.

Now, I was an orphan and it made me feel very alone. I was beginning a frightening journey, overwhelmingly lonely. But I secured a good job in the office of a manufacturing company and my prospects looked good.

***

TIMELINE 1961

"You had a horrific sunburn experience, didn't you?" said Charlie, empting his water bowl.

"Yes Charlie, I did. I was young and I wanted a tan, which was in vogue at the time. It was hot and humid the day I went to the beach to get my "quick" tan. Lake Michigan was a deep blue with the white foam of the waves lapping up on shore. The wind was blowing gently and I could smell the seaweed.

I took my clothes and shoes off trimming down to my swim trunks. I ran along the beach carrying my possessions looking for a good spot. It was exhilarating feeling the gritty sand between my toes. I laid my towel down and flopped on my stomach in the hot sunshine.

Suddenly, I felt a prick in my shoulder. I turned around and saw a figure walking away. I felt woozy and fell asleep.

I remember trying to get up but I was dead weight. I did manage to turn over onto my back. I don't know how long I was asleep but when I did wake up, I noticed Jim Cradock in the distance looking at me.

I felt terrible, my skin was burning, so I put my clothes back on hastily and headed home. Cradock must have injected some sedative into me.

When I got home, my skin on my back and legs was starting to have a painful burning sensation. It was almost unbearable. I ran a tepid bath and just laid in it for an hour. The water relieved the pain. Before I went to bed I applied some Vaseline over my sunburn and it relieved it a bit. What was Cradock trying to do, kill me?

The next day, I went to work with my legs wrapped up in cloths because I couldn't stand my trousers rubbing on my violated skin. It took a long time to get over the damage and pain. But finally, my skin healed. I probably was very close to ending up in the hospital.

I knew now, I would never be safe with Jim Cradock around!

***

CHAPTER SIX

TIMELINE 1963

After all the attacks by Cradock, I've been having extreme anxiety, thinking scary thoughts about what he would do next.

Then one day, I ran into him in the park. I'm sure not by accident, he must have been stalking me.

"Hey look, it's Joe Wiles out for a walk. Fancy meeting you," said Cradock grinning.

"You're trying to kill me aren't you Cradock?"

"No Wiles, you got me wrong. I'm here to make your mind run riot with scary thoughts," said my nemesis, pointing to a bench, "Lets sit down and have a chat."

We sat down.

"Cradock you're messing with my mind. I want you to stop."

He then, kicked my leg.

"Aaaah! That hurt, what did you do that for?"

"What? I didn't know I did anything. You must be imagining things."

"You bastard, there will be a bruise here tomorrow," I said, rubbing my leg.

Cradock started laughing.

"You get a strange joy out of scaring people, don't you?"

"Wiles, your thoughts aren't rational, you're worried for no reason."

"When I see you, I get scary thoughts immediately and that makes it difficult to enjoy my day."

"Good, that's exactly what I wanted to hear."

"My brain interprets all your abuse by giving me anxiety attacks!"

For no apparent reason, Cradock punched me under the ribcage.

"Cut it out or I'll give you one."

"You don't have the guts, Wiles, and anyway you believe in peace at any price!"

"You have a twisted mind."

"My mission is to abuse you for what your grandfather did to my ancestors."

"For the last seventy years or so, the Cradocks have been abusing my family. The Wiles family has taken the Cradocks physical abuse by way of hitting, kicking, and beating resulting in bruises, black eyes, welts, bone fractures and cutting, leaving open wounds!"

"You're crazy Wiles, we've just been scaring you people a little."

Cradock started laughing again, this time it was uncontrollable laughter.

"Scaring people is emotional and psychological abuse in the form of verbal insults, threats, intimidation and harassment."

"Wiles, I will agree with you. I will do anything to make your life miserable, including giving you scary thoughts."

My mind was starting to run riot with all sorts of terrible thoughts about Cradock's actions.

"I will liberate my mind from you, Cradock, if it's the last thing I do."

"Oh yea, how are you going to do that?"

"You've made my mind a prison filled with noisy thoughts because I've left my mind unmanaged. But I will rectify that."

"You will never be able to liberate yourself from your scary thoughts."

With that, he shoved me off of the bench to the ground. Cradock walked away smiling and said:

"I will return, Wiles."

I got up and sat on the bench with my head in my hands. Will I ever get Cradock to see sense and stop the revenge vendetta? Probably not, but I can manage my mind better.

This continual harassment was giving me an anxiety problem. The scary thoughts are becoming severe, I have to shake them, but how?

I could start boxing my thoughts up, separating the ones I want to focus on from the ones I want to dismiss. That would organize my mind. And the thoughts that repeat and repeat might be messengers pointing to something that needs my attention. Maybe it might be time to see if Cradock would be receptive to mending things with forgiveness. I don't know how that would sit with him

****

CHAPTER SEVEN

TIMELINE 1964

Charlie said, "Meeting your wife, Sarah, was a turning point in your life. Tell us about it."

"Yes, that's right, Charlie."

Oh! Oh! I felt that prick again in my arm and I saw a figure in white. I was feeling dizzy. I was getting heart palpitations now, with trembling and shaking. I started sweating with nausea. Following close behind were feelings of detachment and being out of touch with my body. Numbness and tingling sensations followed by hot flushes and then chills. Was I going crazy? I certainly felt out of control…

Then it was 1964 again:

"Would you like to have a date with a girl that just moved into the neighborhood?"

I was taken aback by the question from the proprietor of the corner shop that I frequented, but I said, "Yes, I would."

"She usually comes in for a chat about mid-morning, be here then."

When I got to the shop the next day, a tall good-looking woman was talking to the proprietor. She introduced us:

"Sarah, this is Joe, the fella I told you about."

We smiled at each other. On our first date we went to Lincoln Park and the zoo. The dates that followed were usually seeing movies in the Loop. I only saw Cradock once following us. I didn't mention it to Sarah. I was very happy over the weeks of courting. I think it was after about two months that I had the night to remember.

I took Sarah to a pub/restaurant in the Loop. She looked exquisite that night. Her dark brown hair was draped past her shoulders. She was dressed in a black jacket over a white blouse with black slacks and pumps. The red carnation she was wearing set the whole outfit off.

We sat in a booth opposite each other. I could smell her intoxicating perfume. I looked into her dark soulful eyes and said:

"You look beautiful tonight, Sarah.

"Well, thank you, kind sir," she said smiling.

"What would you like to drink?"

She leaned over toward my face and whispered:

"A margarita, please."

Wow! Sarah had the power to shake me up. I ordered two margaritas.

"Have you been here before?" She slipped off her jacket, her eyes never leaving mine.

"A few times, it's a good place to have a quiet conversation."

We sipped our drinks looking into each other's eyes. Then we ordered dinner and ate leisurely, occasionally smiling at each other. When the dishes were removed, I ordered two more margaritas.

"So, Sarah, are you lonely?" I hoped I wasn't being too blunt.

"No, not really, but I would prefer to be with someone I cared for."

"I hate living alone," I blurted out, "That's why I agreed to our first date set up by the corner shop matchmaker."

Sarah laughed at that remark and then I laughed too.

"When you live alone, you just eat, sleep and work. Life becomes a meaningless joke!"

Sarah stared at me, as if she could see into my soul. And then she reached across the table and held my hand.

"I'm sorry you feel like that, Joe."

"What is your idea of the meaning of life, Sarah?"

She went silent for a few moments and sipped her drink.

"Well, I've always found life a struggle, a predicament that I wished I could control."

I then, spotted Cradock sitting at the bar watching us. It made me angry but I wasn't going to let it ruin the evening.

"I've really enjoyed myself, Joe, these past few weeks."

Sarah smiled coyly and I felt her foot run up and down my calf as she said, "I'm so glad we met, Joe."

"So am I, Sarah."

I glanced at my watch, it was 10 PM.

"Look it's early, we could go over to my place for a night cap. I'll call a taxi, it's only two miles away in Old Town."

"Oh, I'd love to see your house."

I called a taxi and helped Sarah on with her jacket. She whispered in my ear:

"I'm glad we're going somewhere more private."

I felt her breath on my ear, it tickled.

***

I took Sarah's jacket and hung it up and she followed me into the lounge. We stood looking at each other and then Sarah leaned in and tilted her head and I kissed her. We both had our eyes closed and then we opened them slowly and I drew my lips away. She smiled and I kissed her again. This time she opened her lips slightly and I opened mine and then, the tips of our tongues met! It was a long lingering kiss.

"Sit down, Sarah, and I'll make us a drink."

I came back with two margaritas. I put them on the coffee table and sat next to Sarah on the sofa. Her shoes were off. We sipped our drinks and then I leaned over and kissed Sarah's neck. She sighed deeply.

Sarah looked longingly into my eyes as she took off her blouse. I pushed her back on the sofa and removed her slacks. She took off her bra and she was down to her panties. I sat back and marveled at her well-developed body. She got up and took my shirt off, then she pushed me back and pulled off my trousers. Now, she was down to her panties and I was down to my boxers. We smiled at each other and drained our drinks. It was a night to remember...

The next month we decided to get married in the Registry Office since we both had no family. For some reason Cradock didn't bother us for a few years. Sarah and I were deliriously happy. Then Cradock popped up in 1969. He just followed us for a start, being a general nuisance. Sarah thought it was disconcerting but she thought he would stop when we ignored him. But he didn't stop!

***

Charlie said: "Refresh my memory about the boat trip you and Sarah took that was dicey to say the least!"

TIMELINE 1970

It was August and it started out as a wonderful experience. Sarah and I decided to take a two day break, so we booked passage on a ferry/passenger boat going from Chicago, across Lake Michigan, to

Muskegon, Michigan. We would stay the night at the Muskegon end and head back the following day.

The ship loaded up five cars and the passengers and off it went into the blue expanse of Lake Michigan. The boat was about 400 feet long and 50 feet wide. It was to be a slow boat to Muskegon! It traveled about 20 miles per hour. So it took us 5 hours to travel the 120 miles across the widest part of the lake.

About 45 minutes out, land faded away. It was like being in the middle of an ocean! Sarah and I felt like sea explorers, sailing on a boat out of sight of land!

We settled in our deck chairs with some cold drinks. It was very hot and sunny that day. But looking out at the water and observing the gentle movements of the waves made you feel cooler.

"I feel so calm, Sarah, how about you?" I said holding her hand.

"Oh Joe, this is great, the water gives you a sense of calm and clarity."

"The water is so blue today."

"It's my favorite color," said Sarah.

We both smiled as we gazed into each other's eyes.

"The water puts you into a meditative state of mind."

"It's so peaceful out here on the water, it gives you a general sense of happiness."

Sarah laughed, "I feel so satisfied with life at the moment and I'm sure this is triggered by being close to water."

"I think we're hardwired to be happy near water," I said with my eyes closed.

"I like the sound of the waves lapping the sides of the ship."

I looked up at the sky with its puffy clouds and then back at the sea.

"We needed this break, sweetheart, if only to give our brains a rest!"

Sarah laughed.

"I'm serious, we've been working hard lately at our jobs and getting bombarded by the noisy stimuli of busy offices and factories."

Sarah squeezed my hand and we stood up at the railing and looked at the horizon.

"Our brains are at rest now, because there's less information coming in, out here in the middle of Lake Michigan."

I looked around at our fellow passengers, they all had smiles on their faces. We sat down and I stroked Sarah's hair.

"When I'm observing the water's movements, it gives me a mindset of gentle awareness of my surroundings."

"I feel in a state of awe, Joe. I feel a connection to something beyond myself, a closeness to nature."

"I feel closer to you, sweetheart," I said, putting my arm around Sarah.

Life Story Terror

***

We were about two hours into the cruise when I started feeling queasy.

"Joe, you look a little green under the gills."

I felt a cold sweat coming on with dizziness. I went inside the cabin for some relief from the sun. One of the ship's operators told me motion sickness occurs when your eyes tell your brain you're going up and down with the waves. But your inner ear, which gives your brain a sense of balance, tells your brain that you're sitting still! There's a conflict of information.

"Joe, try this, look at a stable object like the horizon and then close your eyes."

"Hey sweetheart, that helped, thank you."

We were about four hours into the trip when I spotted Jim Cradock! This I didn't need, when I was feeling ill.

"Hello buddy, fancy meeting you here," he said, slapping me on the arm.

I felt the sting of sunburn on my arm that I didn't realize I had. With Cradock around it put a damper on the rest of the journey.

Sarah and I disembarked from the ship and rented a room for the night. I felt lousy my sunburn interrupted my sleep.

On the return trip to Chicago, Cradock kept hanging around.

"Did you have a good night's sleep, Wiles?"

"Why don't you leave us alone?" said Sarah in a fighting mood.

"Because your husband's grandfather did a dirty deed on my grandfather."

"We can't be held responsible for something that happened years ago," I chimed in.

"Wiles, you are a blood relative and that means you have to suffer too."

"You're deranged, Cradock," I said, walking toward the railing of the boat.

Suddenly, Cradock came crashing into me, like a bull attacking a red flag!

"Joe, watch out!" Sarah shouted.

I almost flipped over the railing into the sea. Sarah hung on to me. If I went into the water I'm sure I would have been a goner, because I'm a poor swimmer.

"Sorry Wiles, I don't have my sea legs yet!"

It was deliberate, but I couldn't prove it. So a trip that started so wonderful for Sarah and I, ended up terrible!

***

TIMELINE 1975

Charlie wanted to know about the time Sarah and I went to the Sears Tower. It was another day of terror. Sarah and I were enjoying a day in the Chicago Loop and we decided to go to the observation deck on the 103rd floor of the Sears Tower, which was the tallest building in the world at that time.

We got on the express elevator, which was one of the fastest at 1600 feet per minute. I could see the anxious look on Sarah's face, she wasn't keen on elevators. The elevator started its accent and I felt the whoosh through my body. My stomach had a hard time keeping up with me. We got off at the observation deck and Sarah said:

"I wonder if there are stairs to this floor?" Sarah smiled, impishly.

"Yes, I think there are around 2100 stairs to the 103rd floor, but I think I'll stick with the elevator."

We walked around the deck and viewed the city from north, south, east and west. We were ready for our elevator experience again. We got in and in followed Cradock, and the doors shut!

"Fancy meeting you two," he smiled.

And then he pushed the Stop button and we were stuck between floors!

"What are you doing, Cradock, are you nuts?"

Sarah was standing in the corner of the elevator petrified.

"I'm crazy like a fox," shouted Cradock.

He reached into his pocket and pulled out a switchblade knife. He pressed the button and out popped a six-inch blade!

"Come on now, Cradock, my wife is claustrophobic. Let the elevator go down."

The lights flickered in the coffin like contraption.

"Maybe, we'll be here for hours," Cradock snickered.

Sarah snuggled up against me.

"Relax, sweetheart, we'll get out soon."

We were both sweating profusely. I was getting the fear of being trapped. I had the vision of being without food or water with this crazy man in charge. I was trying to remain calm for Sarah's sake.

"Joe, I feel like the walls are closing in on us," cried Sarah.

Cradock kept laughing at our anguish. It was as if we were on a platform dangling over a void of darkness. My imagination was starting to run riot. Sarah was trembling, I had to do something in a hurry. I grabbed Cradock and pushed him to the floor and then I pressed the emergency call button. Cradock managed to cut my arm when I lunged for him. When he started to get up, I pushed him again and he hit his head on the wall and fell unconscious.

Suddenly the elevator started to go down but for some reason it stopped on the fifth floor. The doors opened. Sarah and I ran out and down the stairs. Out on the street we ran to the nearest taxi stand and got a cab home. Sarah bandaged my wound up. Thankfully it was just a flesh wound. But from then on we never knew when or where Cradock would show up!

***

Life Story Terror

Sarah mentioned about getting a restraining order against Cradock. But I pointed out that we would need substantial proof that he was putting us in danger otherwise a judge wouldn't issue the order. Cradock was very crafty in not providing us with hard proof.

***

CHAPTER EIGHT

TIMELINE 1989

"How did Sarah's death affect you after twenty-five years of marriage?" Charlie wanted to know.

My mind drifted away toward another life story memory. Sarah being taken from me all began with what we believed was a chest cold. She had a deep persistent cough for a month. Finally we went to the doctor and he had some x-rays taken. The outcome was that Sarah had lung cancer. She fought against the disease for six months and then just tired out and she passed away at just fifty-one years of age.

The funeral over, I went back to work after a week off. I thought work would be best for me but the nights coming home after work were terrible! Coming home to an empty house was extremely lonely. On top of everything, Jim Cradock found out that Sarah died and started harassing me.

He'd accost me on the street and ask how I felt being alone and tell me how he was glad my wife died. I had to hold my anger in check with all my will power. He told me to watch my back because he always knew where I was. He also said his son, Ed, was out of high school and would be helping him in the revenge vendetta. Was there ever going to be an end to the misery inflicted by the Cradock family?

One day about three weeks after Sarah's funeral, a Macmillan nurse visited me and we had a conversation about grieving and its effects. I didn't tell him about Cradock because the police said I had no proof of harassment and they could do nothing about it.

***

"I'm having a rough time coming to terms with my loss."

"The death of your wife is one of the most painful events you will ever experience," said Dan, the Macmillan nurse, "It can be overwhelming and a very lonely road."

"After twenty-five years together I feel that a big part of me is missing. How can I move toward healing the wound?"

Dan replied after a few moments of thought.

"You have lost a large part of yourself and you're at the beginning of a frightful journey. You need to give yourself time to mourn. Mourning is the expression of your thoughts and feelings about Sarah's death."

There was a hard knock on the front door. When I got to the door, nobody was there. But there was a note on the floor...

"It serves you right to lose your wife." Signed, Your Constant Shadow.

I put the note in the hallway table drawer and returned to Dan.

"Who was at the door?"

"No one, just some kids playing a prank. Lets continue our discussion."

I fell silent for a moment, and then a thought popped into my head.

"I remember one of the last moments I had...," I stopped in mid-sentence, "with my wife."

"Tell me about it," said Dan.

"Well, we were sitting together on the sofa, right before we went to bed...

"Joe, hold me please, and share this time with me," said Sarah, barely audible.

I held her close and said, "Sweetheart, we always shared our lives."

"I know, but now I feel so alone." She started to cry.

I held my wife tightly for a long time. I knew we were losing what was left of our time fast. I started to cry.

"Experiencing the death of Sarah is affecting your head, heart, and spirit. You will have many different emotions as part of your grieving."

"Sometimes I feel like I'm losing control!"

Life Story Terror

We were both silent for a minute, then Dan spoke:

"Joe, you will experience confusion, disorientation, fear, guilt, relief and anger, on top of all this you will feel out of control."

"How can I feel better?"

"Try to treasure your happy memories, these are the best legacies that remain of your wife."

"When I do go over my memories, sometimes it makes me sad."

"Joe, your memories will make you laugh and cry. Your life isn't the same anymore, but you have to go on living while remembering Sarah."

"I still feel so much shock and denial. I feel this can't be happening to me, it seems other people are in the sunshine and I'm in a dark place!"

"Joe, give yourself permission to feel however you feel. It's okay to cry, remember the numbness you feel keeps you from completely falling apart. These feelings have a purpose."

"I feel guilty that I'm still living and have my health."

"You're going to have many mood swings but time is the great healer."

"I want Sarah back, but I know that's impossible."

"That's a normal response to extreme grief."

"I get very frustrated, thinking, WHY did Sarah have to leave me so soon? It isn't fair!"

Dan shook his head and said:

"You have to have some compassion for yourself. You've just lost someone very close to you and it's natural that you find other people's lives less traumatic and that makes you angry. Talk to yourself with sympathy and tell yourself that you won't always feel this way."

I got up and made some coffee for Dan and myself. After we had our coffee, I told him of another change my grief has brought on.

"I had atheistic leanings before Sarah's death, but now they have become stronger than they were after my parent's died. How could there be a god with all the misery I went through?"

"What were you brought up as?"

"Protestant, Presbyterian to be exact."

"Well, it's a personal choice," said Dan smiling.

"Yes, it is, and the more I think about it, there is no evidence that God exists. Science has explained so much about the workings of nature, the earth, and the universe without using God as part of the explanation, that there is no point in believing that God exists."

"Well, if you feel okay with atheism that's great."

"I feel better now that I got rid of all that religious baggage. I believe we live our lives in a linear fashion and everything occurs only once and then they disappear into the past and when you die everything stops!"

After that conversation I never saw Dan again. But that talk helped me.

Charlie barked and the memory was gone.

Life Story Terror

***

TIMELINE 1990

I had Charlie with me one day while I was sitting on a park bench that was Sarah's and my favorite spot. My loss of Sarah was still affecting me deeply even after a year on top of that I had to put up with Cradock's stalking. Charlie had a sad look on his face, as if he really felt for me in my time of trial.

"Is a year the normal amount of time to grieve?" said Charlie.

"I think I needed at least a year to be with my loss before any lessening of grief emotions could be attained."

"Do you talk to Sarah now?"

"Yes Charlie, I have a dialogue with my darling late wife as much as I can."

"What do you talk about?"

"My everyday experiences with a little imagination thrown in."

"Is that part of the healing process?"

Charlie knew how to keep me talking.

"Yes, it is, it helps me to move forward in my life."

Out of nowhere came Cradock and he sat down beside me. Charlie growled.

"What's wrong, Wiles, you look down in the mouth."

"I'm grieving for my late wife."

I was talking to Cradock like he actually had feelings. I should have known better.

"You'll never get over your grief, Wiles. It will torture you forever."

"I was just feeling better and now you come along and spoil it all."

"That's my mission, Wiles, to make you miserable."

Then, I heard a voice in my head:

"Stand up to him, Joe." It was Sarah's voice!

I sensed Sarah's presence. She was trying to give me strength when I wavered.

"Did you hear me, Wiles, I'll always be around to bug you."

"You might be around but you won't bother me as much because I've got a positive state of mind now."

With that, I got up and walked away with Charlie at my heels. I looked back at Cradock and he had a perplexed facial expression. Just remembering Sarah's voice strengthened me. Loss takes away so much, I've had emotional amnesia. Now I remembered that my wife was a strong woman who I relied upon.

And so, Sarah was talking to me and I was talking to her, not in the flesh, but in my imagination. Our conversation had resumed past her death!

***

Life Story Terror

TIMELINE 1993

One day Charlie asked me:

"Tell us about the time you had it out with Jim Cradock."

I felt a prick in my arm again and I saw the white-coated figure. But this memory was clear in my mind even though I felt like I was floating!

It was after my fifth-sixth birthday and I had been living alone for four years. Cradock had been stalking me at various times since Sarah's death. I was getting very angry with the Cradock revenge tactics.

So one day, I decided to face down the monster. It had to be done. It would be cathartic, I could release all my pent up emotions. Also, it would be therapeutic, it would have a good effect on my mind and body.

I knew Cradock didn't open his bar until noon, so I got there at eleven, so we would be alone. I pounded on the door with my fist. The door opened.

"What do you want?" said Cradock, looking like he could kill me.

"Let me in I have to talk to you."

I pushed past him into the musty tavern. I don't know where I got the courage! Cradock slammed the door and bolted it.

"So talk, Wiles."

"I want you to leave me alone and stop following me around."

I was trying to remain calm and keep my wits about me.

"You know I won't stop bothering you, Wiles. It's my mission to make you squirm."

I started pacing back and forth in front of the bar.

"Leave me ALONE! I'm not going to exchange jibes with you. I want to get the message across to you that I want you to leave me alone at all times, for good!"

Cradock stuck his nose in my face.

"You deserve to squirm with fear for the rest of your life."

With that, he pushed me and I stumbled backward.

"I will get legal help to keep you away from me. There will be consequences if you don't leave me alone."

I said this knowing I couldn't prove anything to the authorities.

"You know what, Wiles? I think I'll give you a good beating right now."

Then he pushed me so hard that I fell to the floor. Then he kicked me and laughed. I got to my feet and ran straight for his stomach with my head down like a raging bull. Cradock doubled up and started gasping for breath. I made the mistake of backing off for a moment. He recovered and I saw his fist coming for my face. I didn't duck fast enough. It caught me on the mouth and drew blood.

Life Story Terror

My blood was wet and warm on my face, it tasted like copper in my mouth. Tasting your own blood is a surreal experience. I backed away from Cradock.

Now, I knew I would have to fight as if my life depended on it, because it just might! Cradock was much more muscular than I was. I would have to out maneuver him.

His left shot out and caught me on the side of my face. The punch tore my cheekbone skin. I could see the right cross coming, I sidestepped and threw a punch to his ribcage. He staggered backwards. I grabbed a handful of his hair and pulled his head forward, I lifted my knee and broke his nose! When he retreated I put my shoulder into him and lifted him off the ground and slammed him to the floor. Cradock grunted and went limp. He lay there on the tavern floor with his mouth open and blood running from his nose.

I walked to the door and unbolted it. When I got home I tended to my injuries.

My bruises were sore for two weeks afterwards.

I was never stalked again by Jim Cradock, he died a year later of a heart attack. But his son, Ed, who was twenty-four years old, was left to carry on the vendetta. He sold the tavern and disappeared into the milieu. When and where would he pop up?

Charlie was looking at me with his soulful eyes, so I said to him:

"It's incredible that the Cradocks had been terrorizing the Wiles family all through my life story, starting from my grandfather. Tom Cradock stalked my grandfather, Arthur, until he died. His son, John, terrorized my father, Louis, and turned him into a drunk who stepped in front of a car and got killed. His son, Jim, tried to kill me in the cemetery where my parents were laid to rest, and he stalked me until his death. Now, his son, Ed, was on the loose! Four generations of Cradocks making my life story a tale of Terror!

***

TIMELINE 1998
Charlie wanted to know about my writing career.

When I started writing, I never thought it would result in four books including my Life Story.

"When did you start thinking about being a writer, Joe?" asked Charlie, who was to be my interviewer with me being the interviewee.

"I turned to writing at sixty years old after eight years of living alone after Sarah's death. I retired early because I had enough money from a pension and savings to write full time. I was depressed after being alone so long and I thought writing would be good therapy. I also had a correspondence creative writing course under my belt. But the real motivation was to sum up my life and leave a legacy."

Life Story Terror

"What do you mean by summing up and legacy?" said Charlie, cocking his head and waiting for my answer.

"Well Charlie, I was at the stage of life where I felt an urgent desire to find meaning in my life through the process of looking back and summing up. My legacy is my creative writing that I hope enhances lives now and hopefully will continue to affect people in the future, when I'm gone."

"So, you wanted to write to feel important." Charlie was coming up with some sharp comments!

"I needed to write as if I were important, which I am, to myself! But in reality I'm of no consequence at all. It wouldn't have made any difference in the world if I had never existed!"

"Wow! That's harsh!"

"Harsh, but true."

Charlie looked glum.

"Everything I write about is an opinion of my own. The only thing I'm certain of is that nothing is certain."

"What are your other books about?"

"My first book was about GUILT, the corrosive emotion. The second was about abduction and the relationship between a father and son. The third was about being tormented by a hostile world and searching for peace at different stages of life. And finally, the fourth, as you know, was about the terror in my Life Story."

Charlie wagged his tail.

"They all sound interesting. Didn't Ed Cradock destroy some of your writing once?"

"Yes, I remember it well. I was burning the midnight oil, writing while the inspiration was with me, when I heard a knock on the door. I had no idea how late it was, so I opened the door without checking."

"I'm coming in, Wiles, out of the way!"

Ed Cradock burst past me waving a knife. I didn't know who it was at that moment.

"Get out of my house. Who are you?"

The intruder slammed the door.

"I'm Ed Cradock, son of Jim. I bet you thought I wasn't going to show up and continue the revenge vendetta."

Cradock pushed me down on the sofa and looked at my desk, which was full of manuscripts, two books to be exact. He gathered up all the longhand manuscripts and threw them into the fireplace and set fire to them!

"Burn! Burn!" he yelled.

He was laughing like a madman as we watched my work burn. Then he ran out of the house. I was in tears! I was intending to type them into the computer and save them. Too bad I didn't do it earlier. I never made that mistake again. It took me nearly a year to rewrite the manuscripts. But now, I've got all my books published. I instructed my publisher to give my royalties to charity when I die because I have no family.

Life Story Terror

***

Charlie gave out with a bark. He wanted to know what values guided my life and my writing.

"There are four that guided me:

Integrity, being honest with strong principles. Wisdom, having experience, knowledge and good judgment. Creativity, maintaining my imagination so I can come up with new ideas. And finally, live fully in the present, because it's the only life you have."

"What are some of the things you've learned from your writing?"

"Well Charlie, my old buddy, it has been said that all fiction is partly autobiographical, and I believe it. What I write about has to be felt by me, either in real experience or in my imagination."

"Do you feel close to the characters in your stories?"

"Yes I do, I have empathy with my characters and I identify with them. Like my characters, I can be given to sudden changes in mood or behavior. I can be difficult to understand at times. So, knowing this about myself, I can write convincingly about others."

Charlie was asleep by my side. I, too, felt tired thinking about Cradock burning my longhand manuscripts. Will I ever be free of the Cradock vendetta?

***

CHAPTER NINE

TIMELINE 1999

"Tell me about the time Ed Cradock saved your life?" said Charlie, the curious dog.

"Well, my friend, it was about a year after Cradock burnt my manuscripts. I went fishing off a pier that jutted quite a way out into Lake Michigan. There were a few people around, some were fishing, some just walking the pier for fresh air.

I stood up to re-bait my hook when I slipped, hit my head and fell into the water. At that point the water was about fifteen feet deep. I was semi-conscious but I didn't have the strength to keep my head above water. I remember swallowing a mouthful of water and then I blacked out. When I came to, I was lying on the pier looking up into the face of Ed Cradock!"

Someone said, "You're a hero mister, jumping in and pulling him out before he drowned."

I sat up, coughing. "You saved me Cradock?" I stammered, as the crowd dwindled away.

"That's right, Wiles."

"You mean you're redeeming yourself and your family for making my family suffer through the years? I find that hard to believe."

Ed Cradock laughed that wicked laugh that I had heard before.

"Redemption had nothing to do with it."

"Then, why?"

I stumbled over to a bench and sat down in the sun. Cradock followed me.

"The reason I saved you is because I want you to suffer until you're a very old man. I want to torture you for the rest of your life. I want justice for the Cradocks"

"You're crazy, don't you realize revenge isn't justice."

"Yes it is, Wiles, it's called, "Just Revenge.""

"What you and your family have done through the years is not "just" at all. It's way out of proportion to the supposed "wrong" my grandfather inflicted on your great grandfather."

"Revenge is a kind of justice in my mind, Wiles."

"The trouble with you and your whole family is that you people get a perverse pleasure out of causing the Wiles family to suffer."

"You hit the nail on the head, Wiles. I want the gratification that comes with the Cradock goal being achieved, in other words when you are brought to your knees. I will feel good then!"

"And here I thought you were redeeming yourself and your family by saving me. I thought you were making up for the Cradock bad behavior in the past."

It shocked me that Cradock saved me from drowning. Probably, to keep me alive so he could continue to harass me! So, I thought as long as we were sitting on the beach bench, why not talk to him about the downside of revenge. Maybe, I could change his mind.

"Why don't you give up this useless revenge vendetta that has made my family miserable through the years? I want it to end right here and now. We'd both feel better and we could get on with our lives."

Cradock had that wicked smirk on his face. It was a beautiful day, the water was gently lapping up onto the shore. A peaceful setting but sitting next to me was a man who had a lot of ill will toward me!

Cradock started laughing and he looked at me as if he would like to stick pins in me, like a voodoo doll! I spoke up:

"What motivates you, Cradock?"

"Just hearing the name, Wiles, invokes anger in me. It makes me feel good that I have the power to make you miserable. And most important, I don't ever want the Cradocks to lose face! I will see that there is closure in our favor!"

I shook my head. Would I ever get him to see sense?

"Rather than providing closure, revenge actually does the opposite: It keeps the wound open and fresh!"

"Sometimes, I feel bad about punishing you, but that feeling doesn't last long. I have to make you pay for the past because there's no other way to get justice."

Cradock and I were bitterly apart in our thinking. I was shaken!

"You can't really believe that?" I said, forcefully.

"Yes, I believe I have to rely on my own retaliatory methods."

And with that statement, Cradock gave me an elbow in my ribs!

"Do you always have to react with violence?" I said, rubbing my side.

"That's right, Wiles, when it comes to you, I have an inborn tendency to execute physical damage!"

"Don't you realize that revenge is primitive? It's not civilized. Why act out feelings of hate and make a bad situation worse?"

Cradock gave me another hard elbow in the ribcage, it was starting to get sore. This was a thirty year old man roughing up a senior citizen!

"Stop hitting me in the ribs, don't you have any feeling for older people?"

"I don't care how old you are, Wiles. I believe in an eye-for-an-eye. I'm a fighter and I have no respect for a man who won't hit back."

What could I say to temper his rage?

"There will be costs connected with your revenge that could be devastating to you. You might get some comfort in harassing me but it will be cold comfort. It will destroy your insides."

Cradock just shook his head and said: "I don't believe it."

"Has the word "forgiveness" ever entered your head?"

"In the case of the Wiles family, no, forgiveness is not an option."

"What makes you believe revenge addresses the damage you feel was caused, and that it will be effective?"

"Listen to me, Wiles, this vendetta against you is PAY BACK. It will be effective because of the physical and emotional pain I will slowly inflict on you."

"Cradock, you're talking unreasonably. Your strategy will fail because it attempts to change something that has happened in the past. You can't turn the clock back!"

"It won't fail because every time I attack you, I feel good," said Cradock with a grin.

"Well, I hope you see sense someday because you're NOT increasing your stature by asserting your dominance over me. In the end you're destroying yourself."

"My family has had a grievance against your family and only making your life miserable will rectify it."

I got up and as I was walking away, I said:

"Well, I thank you for saving my life today."

I thought, talking to Ed Cradock was like a tug-of-war exchange!

***

TIMELINE 2000

"You stopped believing in God and turned to atheism. Did you ever discuss this with anybody?" said Charlie.

"Yes, as a matter of fact, I discussed it with Ed Cradock, and we also had a bloody awful fight as well! Cradock believed in God even though he was an evil person!"

"Tell me about it," said Charlie, jumping up and down.

"Well Charlie, atheism has given me courage to live without all that religious baggage weighing me down!"

"But you grew up Christian!"

"Yes Charlie, I was led into it before I started to think for myself."

Charlie laid down and put his head between his paws.

"I remember the time of the atheist discussion and the fight very clearly. I was sitting in the park on one of those benches dedicated to the memory of someone. Cradock came up behind me and flicked my ear so hard I thought it was going to bleed!"

"Hey you, cut it out!" I shouted.

"Hello Wiles, nice day isn't it. God's world is wonderful."

"You believe in God, Cradock?"

"Yes, don't you?"

"I used to, years ago, but when I was about twenty years old I gave up religious belief altogether. I became an atheist, a person who doesn't believe God exists!"

"How can you not believe in God, don't you believe in morality, meaning in life, or human goodness?"

"Now hold on Cradock, don't tell me you believe in those things when you perpetrate such evil things! Dealing with evil people like you would turn anybody off from belief in God!"

"You're nuts, Wiles!"

"No, I'm not nuts. Just because I don't believe in God, doesn't mean I don't believe in morality, meaning in life, and human goodness."

Cradock's face turned mean when he said:

"Anybody who doesn't believe in God deserves a good whack!"

With that he gave me a hard punch on my arm. I grimaced in pain.

After rubbing my arm for a few minutes, I said:

"By the way Cradock, what's your purpose in life and does your God condone it?"

"My purpose is to give you your just deserts and God wants me to get my family's revenge!"

"Do you know for certain that's God's purpose for you?"

"Absolutely! What do you believe?"

"Live and let live, is my motto. I believe we choose our own purposes and goals, and because of that, we are the authors of our own meaning."

Cradock had a mean look on his face when he said:

"Don't you fear death without a belief in an afterlife?"

"No I don't fear death, it's part of the life process. You have a false hope of immortality, but humans are mortal. What you're trying to do is suppress my ideas with persuasion based on fear!"

"Well, I'm happy anyway," said Cradock with a smirk.

"You're one of those peculiar people who derive happiness from behaving despicable."

"You're right Wiles, I'm never happier than when I'm making you miserable!"

Cradock kept mumbling:

"Atheist? How can anybody not believe in God and the afterlife?"

"Because I'm an atheist, I have thrown off childish illusions and have accepted that I have to make my own way in this world."

"Aren't you frightened of the world without a belief in God?"

I shook my head.

"The world is a scary place, but there are opportunities out there to create a satisfying life without supernatural views."

"I'll say it again, you're nuts Wiles."

"The trouble with you, Cradock, is that you live in a world of myth and superstition."

Cradock got up and pushed me to the ground and laughed. I got to my feet and I felt the adrenalin flowing through my body. I hit him on the jaw and he wobbled back and swung a haymaker at me. I turned fast and took the punch on my shoulder. Then I threw three punches, two left jabs and a right straight to his face. He stumbled back, blood trickling from his nose. He looked at me like he thought I didn't have it in me, but I did!

He then kicked me in the back of my leg and I crumpled like a ragdoll. While I was on the ground he gave me a kick in the ribs and then walked away holding his hanky to his nose. At least he now knew I would fight back!

***

Ed Cradock could be very persuasive. I remember the time I went to see an old workmate at the hospital who was dying and because of Cradock's smooth taking he got me kicked out of the hospital room.

"Hello Tim, I thought I'd call in and see you."

He opened his eyes and mumbled:

"Hi Joe, long time no see. Tim's eyes closed.

Life Story Terror

"How are you?" I said, not really knowing what to say.

His eyes opened again.

"Terrible! My mind is foggy and I have pain. They keep me doped up on drugs. Half the time I don't know where I am!" Tim drifted away in sleep.

I sat down in a chair and stared at my friend. Tim's breathing was very labored and discomfort was etched on his pale face. I thought, all those stories you hear about people seeing their whole life pass before them is baloney. When you're in pain and drugged up, you really don't care a fig about what happened in your life.

Even if you did look back from your death bed and think of your "full and rich" life, you would be sick with regret because you would be about to lose everything to death!

I shook the thoughts from my head. I was glad I was here with Tim at the end. But even that moment was ruined by Cradock:

"Will you please leave, I don't want you here," said Tim's sister, entering the room with a nurse.

"But, I'm a friend," I stammered.

"Please leave," she repeated in a firm voice.

I got up and left the room and the hospital reluctantly. Outside, I spotted Cradock, grinning. Whatever he told Tim's sister, it must have persuaded her to push me out!

I walked home tearful.

***

Charlie looked up at me so sadly and said:

"Ed Cradock saved you from drowning, then he tried to kill you, but didn't. Tell me about that incident."

"I was in the Subway station and there wasn't many people around. It's always eerie in the station when you are almost alone. Then I heard the roar of the train coming. I turned around and there was Ed Cradock grinning!

I tried to move away from the edge of the platform but Cradock grabbed me and pushed me ahead of him toward the edge. I was wobbling on the edge when the train whooshed past. My heart was in my mouth!

I turned around but there was no Cradock anywhere to be seen! Three people were at the other end of the platform. They probably didn't see anything. I was very scared, I'll tell you, Charlie."

"I wonder why he is keeping you alive?" said my furry friend.

"Well, I think he wants to let me know he is always around and he wants me to endure many more years of terror."

"It must be hard to write this terror story?" Charlie laid down and stared at me.

"It's cathartic and therapeutic. With the telling, I'm jumping headlong into the abyss! I'm facing down my monsters! But the reward is: a release of pent-up emotions plus telling the story strengthens me in some strange way."

Charlie looked confused.

"There is terror in my story and I can't get away from that. I am isolated in my mind. There are no enfolding arms to keep me safe. I, and I alone, must stand up to my demons!

While I'm writing all this, I'm shouting and weeping onto the page. I'm gripped by anger, pain and fear. I wonder why life has dealt me this terror. What do I do with these extreme emotions? Do I throw a plate across the room and break it into smithereens? It might make me feel better temporarily but it wouldn't deal with the basic problem."

Charlie's eyes were wide open.

"I hope these ramblings of mine answer your question, my friend."

***

CHAPTER TEN

TIMELINE 2001

All of us have memories, fears, terrors and horrors buried inside, which putting them down on paper helps you alleviate. No matter how many frightening things happen in your story, it still pays to go over them. Maybe, you can make some sense of it and find some meaning to it. In the end, your Life Story becomes your Legacy!

"So is it good to tell the stories of our lives no matter how grim and scary?"

said Charlie, rolling over while I scratched his belly.

"It is good to tell the stories to ourselves and others. The masks come off and we know who we are and what exactly happened and why. The stories reinforce the "I" at the center of the accounts."

"What do you mean by "the masks come off"?" Did you ever see a confused look on a dog? Charlie had that look now!

"I call it the Mask Self. We create this self. It is the culmination of all our life experiences, it's our great moments and our traumatic wounds. We create this self to show to the world, and in doing so we protect our vulnerable inner being from the nastiness of the world. It's the lessons we have learned by living life. So, when the masks come off, the truth is exposed."

"I think I understand," said Charlie, scratching his ear.

I laughed watching Charlie's antics.

Charlie barked: "You must feel a lot of gut wrenching when thinking about the Cradock family?"

"Yes Charlie, mental suffering is produced by the telling and writing but it has also alleviated some of the pain. When I'm recalling these events I felt, at the time, like I'd lost control over my life!"

"Can you get control back?"

"Yes, I think that's why writing it down is so therapeutic, after going over your life you achieve a sense of control over, at least, the effects of the experiences."

"So the telling process heals and restores you," said Charlie, licking his paw.

"Yes, that's right, how did I get such a smart dog?"

We both smiled. Yes, dogs do smile!

"The process of writing it all down, clarifies, and makes some sense of it all."

"Your story has terror in it, does it scare you to write about it?"

Charlie's tongue was hanging out. I went and got some water for him.

"Now, to answer your question. Not really scare me exactly, because once written, the story is an object outside of me and I can relate to it in a positive way."

Charlie cocked his head. I knew he understood me.

"You need to feel in control of your story, because if it frightens you too much, your story will control you and make you sick."

"I guess now that you're getting older, this life story telling has great value to you."

"Yes Charlie, I'm rediscovering and connecting up with the person I have always been, I'm unified."

"It unifies you?'

"Yes, it gives me peace of mind and confidence. I have overcome difficulties and this makes me feel good about myself."

"So, you have to explore the darker parts of your life?"

"Yes, I have to face down my monsters!"

Charlie was pacing up and down.

"In conclusion, this life story writing, tells me: No matter what the Cradocks did or do, it will not diminish my enthusiasm."

Charlie gave out with three positive barks!

Life Story Terror

***

"What's it all about, Joe?" Charlie was singing!

"Yes, indeed, Charlie, what's it all about?"

"Tell me," said my little ball of fur.

"Just look at all the people involved through the years, 1890 to the present. First, the Wiles family, my grandfather, my father and myself, then my mother's parents were killed by Janos Kovak, an Austrian army agent, seeking revenge for his bosses.

Then we come to the Cradocks. Tom pursued my grandfather, John pursued my father, and Jim and Ed stalked me, and Ed is still on my tail!

All these people, the perpetrators and the victims, their lives could have been better without revenge feelings. All the years of trying to exact revenge, bit by bit, was it worth it? What purpose and meaning could it have?"

Charlie was itching to say something, I could tell.

"Cradock would say pursuing revenge for his family gave his life meaning."

"Well Charlie, I will say that it's a normal reaction to want revenge when you think you have been wronged. But Tom Cradock and his cohorts were criminals who hurt people physically and mentally. It could be said he and his mates got their just deserts. My grandfather got his revenge by being a stoolie. In the end, wanting revenge is corrosive and not a smart way to live."

"It was and is terrible the way the Cradocks kept pursuing your family," said Charlie, rolling over on his side.

"They want to get a reaction. They want to see how far they can push you and make you miserable."

"They must be very angry people."

"Yes, they are. Their pursuit of revenge fuels their anger. Revenge stops the perpetrator and victim from moving on with their life. They are stuck in the past. I hope it ends someday soon so we can move forward.

***

TIME LINE 2004

I remember once I thought I had ended the vendetta for good but it wasn't to be. I came home from work, opened the front door and Ed Cradock Jumps up from nowhere and pushes his way in.

"Hey Cradock, get out of here!" I shouted.

"Pipe down, Wiles, I just came to rough you up a bit to remind you that I'm still around."

Cradock's first punch glanced off my chin. His second landed on my stomach and doubled me over. The wind was knocked out of me. I tried to stand tall even though my gut ached. Cradock threw a sluggish punch but I managed to duck under it. I gathered all my strength and shot my fist into his ribs. He bent over a bit but didn't fall. He gave me a push and I rocked backward a few steps. This seemed to give him a second wind. He charged me and landed three punches, one to my ribs and two to my head. I fell to the floor.

I stood up and wiped away the trickle of blood coming from my mouth. I stared into Cradock's eyes.

"So, you knocked me down and drew blood. What purpose do you think that accomplished?"

Cradock just laughed and started to walk to the door.

"Hold it Cradock, we could put a stop to all this right now."

He turned around and looked at me with a questioning glare.

"How could we do that, Wiles?"

"Well, your purpose is to make me miserable with this revenge vendetta. My purpose is to try to make you see that revenge makes no sense."

He smirked and said:

"We are what we are and we do what we do. There is no purpose."

"Listen to me please. In this game of life we choose what we want to expend our energy on, the good or the bad. Everyone has the same starting point and life cycle- birth, childhood, adulthood, old age, and death. Our days on this earth are numbered so we have to do things that are good."

"I still want to avenge my grandfather," said Cradock.

"You see that as a good thing but it is a disadvantage to you because it is corrosive."

"I don't buy that reasoning."

"Then try this on for size and think hard on it."

I wiped away more blood from my mouth with the back of my hand.

"Why should I think on it, when I know what makes me feel good."

Cradock punched my arm hard. I flinched, but continued:

"We humans are animals, when someone wrongs us, the automatic nervous system kicks in and we prepare to run of fight."

Cradock had that wicked smirk on his face.

"But, we humans, supposedly, are capable of higher thinking. We try to override our basic instincts. Now you, Cradock, could defuse this situation and we would both be happy. Whether you realize it or not even you could be a victim of your own revenge vendetta."

Cradock gave me a push and said:

"How can I be a victim, you silly git?"

"Because revenge is a corrosive emotion and it will eat you from the inside out."

Cradock glared at me. I had to make my point fast.

"This wrong that my grandfather perpetrated against your grandfather happened in the distant past. I think the vendetta has to do with your ego, you need to save face, if you don't make me suffer, your ego is bruised!"

Cradock laughed and punched my arm again. It was very sore but I wouldn't let him know it.

"You feel it would lower your social position if you let your revenge tendencies go."

Cradock pondered that statement.

"There's a paradox here," I said firmly.

"Oh yea, what's that?"

"By the very act of not taking revenge, you might be seen as a strong person."

Cradock had a pensive look. Was I getting through to him?

"What if I offer an apology for what my grandfather did?"

"My grandfather isn't here to receive it!"

"We all have a time limit on our living, so we must re-evaluate things and choose a different course of action before it's too late!"

He smiled. I might be getting over to him, maybe. I continued while I had him in a receptive mood.

"The purpose of life is NOT to repeat the mistakes our ancestors did, but to rise above it and do as much good in life as we can."

Cradock just stared at me. Then, out of the blue, he said:

"Why did you write your life story? What purpose did you get out of that?"

"Because I am a unique human being with a unique story. I wanted to tell the story so others don't put corrosive revenge over common sense. I wanted to show, that even though there was terror in my story, I still maintained my beliefs, my skills and talents. And even with all the terror I still was a survivor. Finally, I hoped to convince you, Cradock, to quit you vendetta. That would be a triumph for me."

Cradock broke out in loud laughter.

"You'll never stop me continuing the revenge vendetta. You won't have a triumph there, you will have a failure!"

"Our purpose, Ed, yours and mine, should be to enjoy our journey through life."

With that I held my hand out, hoping he would shake it in friendship. Instead he slapped my hand away and pushed me backward so hard that I fell to the floor. He started toward me with hate in his eyes.

I stood up with a wide base with my feet diagonal from each other, something like a martial-arts stance I'd seen on TV. I kicked out at him but he jumped back. I saw surprise in his eyes. Instead of having another go at me, he walked out the door slamming it.

***

TIMELINE 2005

"Didn't you have a nightmare that scared the living daylights out of you?" said Charlie, looking grim.

"Yes Charlie, I can conjure it up in my mind like it was yesterday... I was in bed in a stark white room strapped in some kind of lifting device. In walks all the Cradocks, Tom, John, Jim and Ed, plus another person that I can't quite see in the shadows. Five big men!

"We are here to end your suffering, Wiles."

They all started laughing. It was echoing in my ears. Then out of the shadows came the fifth man. It was Janos Kovac, the Austrian army agent, who killed my mother's parents, my grandparents!

"I'm here to help the Cradocks in their final torture," said Kovac.

I started to sweat from the shock of seeing all these monsters together. Then they all had a go at lifting me up and down continuously for quite a while. They were getting their kicks, and I was getting dizzy. Then they all started poking me with sticks until I almost passed out. Ed Cradock got out a large hypodermic needle.

"When we inject you with this you will sleep forever!"

I started kicking my feet at them but it was futile. They just laughed all the more. As Cradock came toward me with the needle, he said:

"We could let you live a little longer and then we could torture you more. What do you say?"

I thought: Is it better to be alive or dead? Is it better to put up with this torture or fight against it by putting and end to it once and for all? Dying is sleeping, that's all dying is, a sleep that ends all the heartache that life hands us. That's an achievement to wish for!

"Well, Wiles, what's your answer?"

He had his face right close to mind. I spat at him!

"That's my answer, you monster!"

Cradock wiped the saliva from his face and raised the needle…

I woke up in a cold sweat. Thankfully I never had that nightmare again. I wondered what Freud would have to say about it.

"Oh boy, writing your life story really had a scary effect on you," said Charlie soberly.

I petted Charlie with long strokes down his fury body.

"Before I began to write my story, I didn't realize the effect the past had on my present. Because of the Cradock's revenge vendetta and the terrible thing that happened to my maternal grandparents, I was literally writing myself into the darkness."

"What was your big fear?"

"The fear of facing events on paper from the painful past."

"Did the writing help you find yourself?"

"Yes, it did, there is only one of me and my voice is unique so the mask came off and my true self was revealed. If I didn't express myself and explore the person I am, the essence of myself would be lost forever!"

"So, you're glad you wrote your life story?"

Life Story Terror

"Of course, writing my story, even though it was full of terror, was a way of removing the muzzle and blinders of fear and expressing myself. Writing forced me to examine my life and the revenge vendetta of the Cradocks."

I looked at Charlie, he was staring at me intently.

"I didn't want fear to stop me from writing "Life Story Terror". After years of silence, I now had a voice!"

***

CHAPTER ELEVEN

TIMELINE 2012

Charlie's eyes looked sad when he asked:

"When did you feel OLD and have the fear of losing it?"

"Probably right now, at 74, things seem to be falling apart. My panic attacks are more frequent. My days are humdrum or worse. I rattle around this two bedroom bungalow dwelling on my mortality. I have strange thoughts like:

I want to die with my eyes wide open! I don't want anyone to slide my eyelids shut, like they do in the movies. Nobody has to fear making eye contact with me after I'm dead. People that are superstitious would fear looking at my eyes for fear I'd take them with me."

"Living alone must be getting to you after so many years without Sarah?"

"That's right, Charlie. It's scary to realize my own mortality. The last panic attack I had was like a physiological earthquake. They are traumatic and debilitating. I can be calm one minute and then I start a progression of degrees of anxiety, right up to the full blown attack."

"What is a full blown attack like?"

"I experience heart palpitations, breathing difficulties, dizziness, fear of going crazy and dying."

"Boy, that's a scary list," said Charlie, whimpering, "Can you really die or go crazy from a panic attack?"

"When my panic attacks started, I asked the doctor that question. He enlightened me: As far as dying goes, during an attack it just feels like a heart attack because your chest muscles hurt as a result of your shallow breathing. You're not going crazy either, it just feels that way because of your extreme anxiety."

Charlie was whimpering again.

"You said you were falling apart, what's that all about?"

"Well, my fury friend, ageing is all about our parts wearing away. I've noticed I don't chew my food as good as I used to. The bones and muscles of my jaw are becoming porous and weak. As we age, the calcium seeps out of our skeletons and into our tissues, our blood vessels and muscles also get stiff. My legs are giving out because of muscle wastage. I'm always afraid of falling."

"You're describing the pathway to decrepitude and frailty!" Charlie had a concerned look on his face.

"Well, our cells are constantly regenerating themselves. But there comes a time when one too many joints are damaged and too many arteries calcify. There are no more backups that repair. So, we wear out and shut down. In other words, we just fall apart. Decline is our fate!"

Charlie was scratching behind his ear.

"Well, with everything falling apart, the next question is: Would you be happier believing in God?"

"I don't think so, Charlie. People that believe in God base their belief and persuasion on FEAR, the normal fear of death and leading on from that, the trumped-up fear of Hell and eternal torture. They base their belief on a false hope of immortality in some Heaven. But, belief is a personal choice, if that makes them happy, fine. But, I believe in the cycle of Nothingness-Birth-Life-Death-Nothingness!"

"What do you believe, that makes you comfortable even in the midst of the ageing process?"

"I'm constantly trying to know myself better. The more I discover about myself, the more personal growth I have. I also always face my fears. Taking action in the face of fear gives me courage to keep going on and living fully. And finally, I try to celebrate who I am. I try to accept all of who I am, my light side and my dark side. I am a unique person, there will never be anyone exactly like me again. So, I want to live productively with confidence and fulfillment."

"Do you have ideas and things that help you along the way?'

"Yes I do, and here are some of them:

I try to do something I enjoy every day and that's writing. I try to learn new things. All my life I've been dabbling in Philosophy. It exercises my brain. I have a special place, a refuge, to do my writing. This makes me happy because it is uniquely mine. I call it my Scriptorium.

I laugh as much as possible even with the Cradock vendetta going on. It releases endorphins, the feel-good chemicals. I meditate daily and try to embrace old age. I'm older and supposedly smarter and more experienced and I have more time to do the things I enjoy.

And finally, I keep my mortality in the forefront of my mind. It helps me appreciate every day and I try to get the most out of it. Looking over your shoulder at your own death is a great motivator!"

***

Charlie said: "What age do you feel at this moment?"

"At this moment in my head, I feel twenty, ready to take on life and all it's wonders. The mind is willing but the body isn't. But really Charlie, it varies. Some days I feel like I'm twenty and just disguised as an adult. I pretend old age isn't here but when I feel pain in my joints, I know different."

"How are you physically?' Charlie took a drink from his bowl.

"Physically, as I told you, it's a slippery slope downwards. I have to amend that statement, on the whole it's up and down. If I rise in the morning not feeling much pain, I fell forty or fifty. I take you, Charlie, on walkies with a slight limp.

But there are mornings I get up full of aches and pains and despair. Those days I feel a hundred! And when I look in the mirror with no clothes on, oh, what a horror show! So, I don't look in the mirror too often.

Most mornings, I wake up knowing that one day it's all going to end, but I keep pushing on. That's all we can do!"

"How's your mobility?"

"Boy Charlie, you want to know everything. Well, I have a cane that I rely on. I'm very wobbly so it's hard not to fall over. Sprains and bruises take longer to heal. All this tends to remind me that the Grim Reaper is getting closer."

"What do you fear most about old age?"

"Dementia and ending up in an old people's home."

"Even though you are harassed by Ed Cradock, how do you keep a sense of perspective and stay alert in mind and spirit?"

With the knowledge that the Cradocks have been popping up over the last one hundred years, it's hard to keep a sense of perspective. I do a lot of grumbling and complaining, but I like to keep to some kind of "thinking schedule", to keep me on the straight and narrow. In other words, to keep my sanity!"

"Thinking schedule?" said Charlie, looking quizzical. Yes, dogs can look quizzical!

"With people like the Cradocks wandering around the world, I struggle to understand the meaning in the world. As someone once said:

"It's like walking around a huge library without touching the books."

Do you want me to list my "thinking schedule?"

"Yes please." Charlie is a very curious dog!

"To begin with, writing about your problems is a great help. You are doing your thinking on paper, you are seeing things from a new and clear point of view. I take walks with you, Charlie, which helps quiet my thoughts so it's easier to get things in perspective.

I ask "Why" to a lot of things to get a clear picture and maybe open up the possibility of change. I listen to the other side of arguments. I tried many times to reason with Cradock."

"Anything else?" Charlie was pushing again.

"I often thought: How can I grow old without feeling old?"

"Did you come up with some answers?" said Charlie, the dog with an inquiring mind.

"Yes, I try not to worry about my age. This age number does not define who I am. What does define me is how I think and what I do.'

Charlie was making slurping noises drinking from his bowl.

I continued: "My writing has been a great boon to me. It keeps my mind alert and I get satisfaction from stringing words together. Also, I had to get a computer and learn how to use it. It was a great help with my writing and research. The internet has brought the whole world into my writing room."

"So, thinking about all these things keep you sane and young in mind."

"That's right Charlie, I don't want to give people the impression of me as a "poor old thing."

***

"So, are you lonely?" said the thinking man's dog.

"No, I'm not. I live in this bungalow alone with you, my dog. I don't get visitors but that's okay. I love peace and quiet in my declining years. You could say, I now prefer SOLITUDE."

"So, what brought you joy?"

"I had some joy with my parents in my childhood and then as an adult. I had joy with my wife Sarah. And finally, I had joy in creating fiction in my novels."

Charlie looked agitated and said:

"I don't like to be alone."

"Charlie, we are all alone, we were born alone, we die alone and in spite of all the people we've had around us all our lives, we are alone on the whole of life's journey!"

Charlie nodded his head and then curled up and went to sleep.

**

TIMELINE 2013

I heard a knock on the door. I moved too fast toward the door and fell like the decrepit old man I was. I hurt my leg and crawled to the door and opened it. There stood Ed Cradock looking down at me. He rammed his way in and slammed the door.

"Hello Wiles, thought I'd give you a visit. What's wrong with your leg?"

"I just fell."

"Oh, I'm sorry." He then kicked my leg. The pain was searing.

He dragged me into the lounge and lifted me onto the sofa. Charlie started barking. He grabbled his collar and pulled him into the bedroom and closed the door.

"What do you want from me?" I mumbled.

Cradock laughed and said:

"I've been observing your bungalow for the last year and I've noticed you get no visitors and you don't go out much."

"So what, I'm an old man living alone."

"That's just it, Wiles, I think you're ready for the Old People's Home!"

"You're nuts, get out of my house. I'm not afraid of you anymore, my atheism has given me boldness and courage."

"I'll leave when I'm finished with my evaluation of how you are managing the activities of your daily living."

"What do you know about evaluating me and my daily activities?"

I tried to stand up but I couldn't put weight on my injured leg. I fell back on the sofa in pain.

"You see, you can't even walk. Anyway in the last year I've taken a carer's course, so I do know how to evaluate whether you should be living alone or not."

"I wouldn't want you to take care of me." I was squirming with pain on the sofa.

"Get me some help, the pain is terrible," I yelled.

"When I'm finished with the evaluation I will call an ambulance."

Cradock smiled, that wicked smile of his, and took a long look at me.

"Now, lets see, you are starting to have falls in the house. As people get older falls happen on a regular basis. I can see you've lost weight. You've probably not been eating regularly. You have wrinkled and stained clothes on and you've not shaved in days. You obviously don't care about your appearance anymore."

Life Story Terror

He walked over to my mail basket and saw lots of unopened post. Next he entered the kitchen and came back five minutes later.

"You've got stale and expired foods in the fridge. Some of your pots and pans have singed bottoms and your potholders are burnt on the edges!"

He went further into the lounge.

"There's lots of dust around, it's obvious you don't do much cleaning."

Cradock kicked a book and some papers on the floor.

"Lots of clutter and cobwebs all over."

He shook his head and gestured all over.

"Well Wiles, my considered opinion is that you need to go into a care home immediately. You definitely can no longer live alone."

By this time my leg had started to swell and the pain was almost unbearable.

"Please call someone, I need medical assistance."

Cradock called an ambulance and walked out the door. I crawled over to the bedroom and let Charlie out. The ambulance came and took Charlie to a kennels and me to the hospital.

I came home a week later with a zimmer frame, the hospital lent me. I had a lower leg fracture, the doc fixed me up with a splint. The doc also said I couldn't remember my name at first when I was admitted to the hospital. He made an appointment for me to take a dementia test.

Charlie was returned to me from the kennels. I was glad to see him. He was my buddy and confidant.

***

"How did you get on after the dementia test?" Charlie was visibly concerned.

"Well Charlie, I went through a written test and a brain scan. The diagnosis was I'm in the early stage of Alzheimer's disease."

"I'm sorry to hear that, How fast does it progress?"

"Well, I'll tell you, Charlie, I'm glad to have you back because you are a source of inner strength for me when I face bad news," I patted his head, "The doc told me, that on average the disease can progress to the late stage in five to eight years."

Charlie looked devastated, just like I felt.

***

I heard a knock at the door.

"Who is it?" I said through the door.

"Mailman, I have a package too big for the letter drop."

I opened the door a crack and Cradock pushed in knocking me down.

"Get out of my house," I shouted, getting to my feet.

Cradock grabbed my arm and led me to the sofa and pushed me down. He shut Charlie in the kitchen.

"Well Wiles, they fixed your leg but I've heard you were diagnosed with Alzheimer's," he smiled.

"How did you find out?"

"You forgot! I'm a professional carer now. I find out lots of things in my travels."

I could hear Charlie barking in the kitchen.

"Now Wiles, you're not only falling apart physically, but also mentally. You definitely will be going into an old people's home before long."

"How can a brute like you be a carer?"

"I have a light side along with a dark side," he laughed.

I got off the sofa and tried to hobble to the backdoor but Cadock caught me and dragged me back to the sofa. I was so scared I could hardly breathe. It was like someone was choking me. My heart was racing and all I wanted to do was curl up into a ball. No one was going to save me, I lived alone. I could feel my pulse beating in my ears. My hands started shaking. I couldn't control them.

Cradock came closer to me. He took a rope out of his pocket and grabbed my wrists and started winding the rope around them.

"What are you doing?" I gasped, "Are you going to leave me tied up so I starve to death?"

Cradock just laughed as he proceeded to tie my ankles. I noticed he wasn't tying me so tight, probably just enough to keep me immobilized for a while. Another way to torture the old man!

"Now listen, this is what you will have to go through in stages: memory loss, losing things, communication problems, loss of mobility, incontinence, difficulties in eating and drinking, infections, not to mention all your other ailments. Well, how do you feel about that Wiles?'

"I feel numb and very angry. Anger that I have to put up with you and this debilitating disease at the same time. I'm sad and depressed about the way my life is changing."

Cradock was laughing again.

"I'll call the police when I get out of these ropes."

Cradock kicked my leg, the pain was crippling.

"Ahhhhg! You bastard! Leave me alone."

"The police wouldn't believe you, you have no proof."

"Get out! Get Out!"

"I'm leaving but I might have social services visit you in the near future."

He walked out of the house laughing.

After an hour, I worked out of my ropes. I was sore and stiff.

***

CHAPTER TWELVE

A month later...

"Charlie, as the days go by, I'm noticing my decrepitude increasing and my dementia creeping up on me."

"In what ways?" said Charlie.

"The other day I couldn't remember the date or what day it was and I seem to be wringing my hands a lot lately. In the mornings I struggle to get out of bed because my joints are stiff. When I go out for a walk my legs give out after five minutes. I used to love to travel, but now, my body says NO, because I don't have the energy for the hours in airplanes of airports. I can't explore city streets or the countryside because of my weak legs. I feel my shelf life is coming to an end!"

"It all sounds so depressing," said Charlie, sadly.

"It's a sad reality of the aging process plus the dementia. With the aches and pains getting worse and memory loss increasing, I don't want to endure the indignity of the last stage of deterioration. Maybe I should be thinking of self-deliverance! I want control, my body is mine."

"What is self-deliverance?" said Charlie, looking worried.

"Some people want to live to their last breath, no matter how grim and painful, and that's their right. But I do not, and that's my right. Self-deliverance is the act of taking your own life to escape the suffering you do not want to bear."

"I understand what you are talking about, but I am shocked," said Charlie, looking up at me lovingly.

I laughed, "Don't be shocked. This is what I would want if I couldn't bear my physical and mental condition. Anyway, after I'm dead for a year and emotions are under control, have a party. Funerals are so barbaric!"

***

I heard a noise in the back of the bungalow and the next thing I was looking at was Ed Cradock!

"See Wiles, you're losing it, you left the back door open so anybody could walk in!"

"You're trespassing Cradock, get out!"

He laughed and shoved me down on the sofa.

"I'm going to get a social worker to visit you soon and we'll get you to an old people's home, for your own good."

Cradock looked for my reaction.

"Maybe, I won't be here."

Cradock got loud then.

"You're not thinking of suicide, are you?"

Charlie started barking.

"Shut that mutt up or I'll shut him up!"

I took Charlie and put him on my lap.

"Are you going around the bend already Wiles? Don't you know suicide is a cowardly and emotionally disturbed act?"

Now, it was my turn to laugh.

"You mean I'd be denying you your pleasure at seeing me suffer. Is that it Cradock?"

"No, I just want you to be comfortable in a care home. I'm thinking of your best interests."

"You're full of baloney and you know it!"

I couldn't help but laugh again.

"My self-deliverance would rob society of its traditional values that have been reinforced by accepted mores, beliefs and attitudes. It's impossible for you to believe that a free-thinking person would ever end it all, regardless of life's debilitating and dehumanizing pressures!"

Cradock shook his head, his face flushed with anger and then he exited the way he came in.

***

"Can you sum up all the revenge tactics that the Cradocks have inflicted on you and your family?" Charlie has his serious face on.

Yes, dogs have all the facial expressions that we have.

"Charlie, that's a broad question, where should I start?"

"Start with your paternal grandfather."

"Well, yes, it all started with my grandfather, Art Wiles. Tom Cradock stalked Art from 1890 through to his death in 1922. This made Art's life very miserable at times. Tom Cradock died soon after Art but that didn't end the revenge vendetta."

"Now it was your father's turn to be on the receiving end of the vendetta."

"That's right Charlie, Tom's son, John, took over the vendetta. He exacted his revenge by stalking my father, Louis, driving him to drink which ruined his family life. Then when John died, his son, Jim, took over."

There was a reflective silence for a couple of minutes.

"Now, it was my turn to feel the Cradock's revenge. And, unfortunately, my wife, Sarah, had to endure it too. My mother also felt the sting of revenge when her parents were killing in a fire set by Janos Kovac."

"And this revenge vendetta is continuing into your old age," said Charlie.

"That's right, Jim's son, Ed, is continuing the terror. He's even interfering in my ageing process by getting me put into an old people's home!"

"Do you think you'll ever get your own back on the Cradocks?"

"I don't know, Charlie, it doesn't look good with me going to a care home."

"This revenge vendetta is like a web that tangles you up," said Charlie.

"Right you are, Charlie. Revenge is vigilante justice perpetrated by a person who takes it upon themselves to punish people for a supposedly injustice without any legal authority."

"The perpetrator probably isn't in their right mind!"

"You are right on the button, Charlie, revenge is an act of strong emotion that clouds the perpetrator's mind. The Cradocks thought their vengeance was an act of justice. But was it right to exact misery on so many people? Now, Ed Cradock thinks he is getting revenge on the Wiles family for a wrong committed a hundred years ago! But I think it is a crime what he is doing."

"Well, I guess that sums it up," said Charlie, snuggling next to me.

"Yes, tomorrow I will be taken to the old people's home! Why does life have to end so ignominiously?"

"Boy, that's a long word!"

"Yes Charlie, it is, but it's the right word. It means full of shame and indignity."

***

TIMELINE 2015

The next day the social worker came to evaluate me. Maybe I would have a few more days before they took me in. During the evaluation I tripped on a throw rug and hurt my arm. Now, I was struggling to make coffee for myself!

"I don't want to go to a care home because I'm afraid."

"Mr. Wiles, there's nothing to fear," said the social worker.

"I want to stay in my home."

"No, you can't stay in your home, you can't cope anymore."

My anger was rising.

"I hate it when people say, "NO" all the time.'

"Mr. Wiles, you don't have the ability to handle your situation."

"I can't stand it when people doubt my abilities. It makes me angry."

"Mr. Wiles, I've only got your best interests at heart."

She packed up my clothes and some personal items and said:

"It's time to go to your new home."

I remained seated on the sofa.

"I'm not going!"

In the end, she got two burly men in white coats to drag me out and put me into a white van.

***

I was in the care home whether I liked it or not! My pension was taken and my bungalow sold to pay for my keep. My life story would end in the old people's home!

"How did you get settled in the home?" said Charlie, sitting on his hind legs.

That's the last thing I remember Charlie asking me. They took him away. No dogs in the home!

"I brought some of my books and memorabilia to make my room more personal. The carer unpacked my case and put my clothes in a wardrobe.

"Are you my carer?"

"No Mr. Wiles, I'm not your key carer. He's not here yet."

I wondered what my key carer would be like. The initial greeter carer gave me a tour of the place in a wheelchair. As we went along the hallway, I heard some commotion from one of the rooms, all of a sudden the door opened and I saw a white clad carer holding a woman's arms while another was putting food in her mouth. The carer that was pushing me quickly shut the door.

"What was that all about?"

The carer smiled and said:

"Sometimes the residents get awkward and we have to aid them in eating."

I thought: How awkward could a frail woman, probably in her late eighties be?

We continued down the hall... From another door I heard some moaning. The door was half open and I saw a man sitting on a chair slumped over his chest.

"What's wrong with him?"

"That's Jehovah, he just sits for hours moaning. He doesn't usually want to do anything."

I shook my head.

Then we passed a room where a woman was sitting facing the wall with her head down.

"How come she's facing the wall?"

"She does a lot of screaming, but when she faces the wall she is quiet," said the carer.

We got back to my room and the carer helped me to a chair by the window. I reflected on what I had just witnessed in my short time in the home and frankly it really scared me!

"Hopefully, things will get better," I said to myself. I had to make myself feel good because I was a prisoner here now!

Then a lady patient in a wheelchair came in and told me:

"This place offers the basic service of keeping you alive!"

"I realize that after what I just saw," I said.

"My name is Jenny, by the way. I'm not supposed to be here talking to you, but I feel compelled to tell people the horrors of this care home. I've always been scared of the thought of being in one and here I am."

I looked sadly at Jenny, she was very thin and her face had a grey colour.

Life Story Terror

"People here ignore me, but I tell the truth. A few days ago my legs gave out and I was stuck in bed. The "so called" carers put water and food in my room but it was placed where I couldn't get it. I couldn't get to the call button so I ended up with a parched throat and very hungry."

"I can't believe things here are that bad."

"What's your name?"

"Joe Wiles."

"Well, I'll tell you Joe, I wish before I was put here I had a stash of drugs so I could have ended things my way instead of left in a bed thirsty and staving!"

Jenny kept looking around to see if anyone was coming. She was actually frightened of being discovered talking to me.

"I have so much pain with my arthritis and they make me sit in a chair but because I'm so thin, I'm sitting on bone, which is extremely painful. I have to wear diapers now, but this place has a quota for diapers. So, when I haven't filled my diaper completely, you get wiped and it's put back on. What do you think about that?

"That's terrible."

"It's all very frightening, Joe. They've started housing old psychiatric patients here now. They just mix them in. I better go, I hear someone coming. Don't tell anybody I was here."

Jenny wheeled herself out fast. A minute later my carer came back.

"Are you okay, Mr. Wiles?"

I started crying, the carer gave me a box of tissues. They must have been the cheapest tissues they could buy because they were very scratchy on my nose and face.

"Mr. Wiles, your medication is going to be changed right away."

What Jenny told me was racing through my mind when the carer told me about the change in medication. I thought that a rapid change wouldn't be so good because there could be side effects and sometimes the change could be dangerous!

***

The first morning, the carer woke me up:

"I can't see!" I shouted.

"Come on, Mr. Wiles, get a move on," said the heavy-set carer.

When I got moving my vision straightened out just before I was about to walk into a wall.

"What's wrong with you," said the carer, "You're eyes are shut."

I then realized my eyelids were barely open. I felt very dizzy. The carer grabbed my arm and led me back to bed.

"That new medication you gave me last night must have drugged me. The side effect is making me dizzy."

Life Story Terror

"You're wrong, Mr. Wiles, the doctor said this is the med you need."

"But I'm feeling bad side effects!"

The carer shook her head and gave me a grim look. I know she didn't like what I said.

***

A little later they let me wander around the halls. I saw a few carers at the desk and I stopped to say I didn't feel good, but they ignored my presence and went on with their conversations as if I didn't exist. It was like they didn't need to respond to me because I was one of the "crazy" ones!

As I walked the halls there were noises of moans and groans coming from the rooms. It was never quiet! I saw carers running back and forth between wards. I stopped one and stammered that I didn't feel well.

"I'm busy right now, we're short staffed. If you want to talk to somebody go to the desk."

"But I've just been there and got no response!"

The carer hurried away. I walked down the hall avoiding some patients that looked a little scary. I got back to my room and sat down. I was over medicated so I could hardly move. I was in a stupor.

That day made me realize it wasn't the patients to be scared of, it was the staff! Two days here and I felt like a zombie in a place that seemed unreal.

***

CHAPTER THIRTEEN

"Wake up Mr. Wiles, it's 6 AM," said the nurse.

I rubbed my eyes and looked around the room. I had some of my personal effects there, which was comforting. I was told I was in the "living" section of the home. There also was a "dying" section where the inhabitants don't go out of their rooms. They are checked every three hours to see if they are still breathing, to change their incontinence pads, to puff up their pillows and wet their dry lips.

"I have to go to the toilet," I mumbled.

"Well, Mr. Wiles, you know where it is," said the nurse, straightening up my bed.

I walked out of my room very unsteady on my feet. My bare feet hit the cold tiles. I forgot to put my slippers on. As I was walking, I realized how quiet it was in the long hallway. I smelled a strong odor of disinfectant. The light above was flickering. Everything in the hallway was a shade of white, the floor the walls, the ceiling, even my nightgown. Suddenly, I heard yelling coming from the toilet. I burst through the door and there on the floor was a resident of the home. Two burly care workers were standing over a frail lady, one slapped her face twice and then started to shake her violently.

I'm sorry you had to see this, Mr. Wiles, but Sophie here, is acting up."

Sophie was eighty-nine years old and just skin and bone, I wondered how much she could act up! They dragged her back to her room. I did my business and limped back to my room in a daze.

"Mr. Wiles, your bed was damp this morning, I think we will have to start putting incontinence pads on you at bedtime."

I climbed on the bed, I noticed there was a rubber sheet on it.

"Take your nightgown off, I'm going to give you a sponge bath," said the male nurse.

The fat carer was very rough with the sponge. My skin was red and sore. He then dressed me and sat me in a wheelchair. He wheeled me into the day room.

"Morning John, I wonder what's for breakfast?"

"Probably the same monotonous stuff. Orange juice, cereal and coffee," said John, staring into space.

In this care home there were forty residents, half men and half women. We were brought our breakfast on a trolley. John was right, it was boring.

10 AM

"Time for your medicine, Mr. Wiles."

I had no idea what they were giving me. Probably high blood pressure pills, which I was taking before I came here. Also, I think they load us up with antidepressants. They say the drugs will help us cope with being here. But I think it's to counter our suicidal tendencies. One of the residents tried to kill himself by hanging, using the "help" bell cord that are in every room.

10:30 AM

"Want a cup of tea, Mr. Wiles?"

"Yes please." I didn't feel like tea, but it was something to do.

There wasn't many in the day room, some prefer to stay in their private quarters. Today, I am at a table with three men who I usually chat with, but today they are all asleep in their chairs. So I read a newspaper.

After a while, I laid the paper down and looked around the room. Four women and one man were sitting in chairs pushed against a wall. They were all silent. This group were the very frail and feeble bunch that the carers kept together.

I spotted a chap in the corner, Tom, I think his name was, sitting with his hand propping up the left side of his face, like he just was told some terrible news. But, ten minutes later, he was still in the same position. It became clear to me that he was not in shock, but simply asleep.

"It's the monotony, all we can do is sleep," said the gent next to me, just waking up.

Life Story Terror

11 AM

"It's about time they opened some windows," said the man called Jehovah.

I don't know if that's his real name or if he thinks he is God!

"Yes, they're just opening them now, it's nice to get some fresh air," I said, smiling at God.

Just when I was inhaling some fresh air, they wheeled me into the TV room.

The corridors had the smell of urine. It's not surprising since only about half the residents can go to the toilet independently! I fell asleep watching TV.

NOON

"Lunch time Mr. Wiles, wake up!"

I opened my eyes to see a nurse tying a bib around my neck. Lunch was tuna pasta with some vegies.

"That was good, wasn't it, Joe?" said the nurse as she took away my tray. Some carers called you by your first name and some always used "mister".

"Now Joe, what would you like for lunch tomorrow?"

I decided and said: "That's what I will have if I'm still alive!"

The nurse walked away as if she never heard me!

1:30 PM

"Wouldn't it be wonderful if we could go out in the garden?" said Mabel, looking wistfully out the window.

"The nurse told me it was too dangerous because the garden was overgrown and the shrub branches would scratch us," I said, knowingly.

"Being in the garden is good therapy. Why did they let it get overgrown? I used to like my garden."

We both sat staring out at the greenery.

3 PM

"Look, we're the only people awake in the day room," said Jehovah.

He was right. There were ten people in the room, including us, eight were snoring in their chairs, their heads flopped over their chests like rag dolls.

"Yes Jehovah, it's a scene of joyless inertia. It symbolizes the function of this place: a place where old people are left to die!"

"I was hoping my sister would visit me today, but she rarely comes now. It just shows blood isn't thicker than water." Jehovah looked sad.

"Blood means you are related, but loyalty is what matters," I pontificated.

"My sister is just like a stranger to me now."

"Sometimes, Jehovah, you have to accept the fact that things will never go back to how they use to be."

Jehovah shook his head.

"It doesn't seem to matter if she comes or not now," said God.

"The reason for that, Jehovah, is: If a person's presence doesn't make an impact then their absence won't make any difference."

We both ended up staring into space.

5:30 PM

"Sandwiches tonight, Mr. Wiles," said a heavy-set nurse I haven't seen before.

"I don't want any," said a gent in the corner.

"They're good for you," said the carer, putting a bit into the gent's mouth.

I ate my sandwich fast, I didn't want to be force fed. I pulled off my disposable bib and crumpled it up and threw it in the bin. Some residents were wheeled to their rooms early. I stayed in the day room reading my book. No one was talking, some were sleeping, or maybe they were drugged.

8:30 PM

We are all in our rooms now, watching TV in bed. In the hall I can hear the sound of choking coughs and other TV's on high volume. The night nurses are handing out the last pills of the day. I think mine are antidepressants. There are some screams in the corridor, it was the people with pain being given their strong painkillers. In my mind's eye, I could see those poor things with no teeth and their faces fallen inwards where their mouth used to be. Their eyes are closed, but there is a moan to be heard.

My last thought before I drop off to sleep is:

"Ageing is natural but it can be very nasty!"

The days go on in monotony.

***

Then one day at 6 AM:

"Wake up, Wiles, time to get you up."

I opened my eyes slowly. I recognized that voice. When my eyes focused, I was looking at the face of Ed Cradock!

"Don't hurt me, please, I'm an old man. Oh, no, it can't be you," I stammered.

I though I heard Charlie bark, but he disappeared years ago, I think.

"What do you mean? Hurt you? I'm here to help you Wiles, I'm your carer! Now get out of bed and I'll get you dressed and put you in your wheelchair."

When I got out of bed my legs collapsed and I fell to the floor! Cradock lifted me into my chair.

"God, you're heavy, we're going to have to use the hoist for you from now on."

"What's wrong with my legs?"

"Looks like muscle atrophy, a wasting away of the muscles in the legs. It comes from lack of exercise in old age."

Cradock pushed me to the day room and left.

"Another day of monotony," said Jehovah, staring at the ceiling.

I nodded my head and asked a nurse about Cradock and she said"

"Mr. Cradock is a fully accredited carer and he is assigned to you Mr. Wiles."

This place wasn't bad enough, now I had the sadist as a carer!

After lunch, Cradock wheeled me back to my room. I had my eyes closed when I felt a pin prick on my arm, just like I felt when telling Charlie my life story incidents. I opened my eyes and there was Cradock, smiling.

"You will relax now, Wiles."

And then, I drifted off into blackness.

***

I woke up and I tried to get out of my wheelchair but my legs wouldn't let me. I pulled the help cord. I had to go to the toilet but no one came for five minutes! I pulled the cord again. The wall clock said 4 PM. I had been out for over four hours! I felt very weak. Finally, Cradock came.

"What do you want, Wiles?"

"I have to go to the toilet."

After the toilet break, Cradock gave me another jab and I fell asleep again. I woke up at 8 PM, another four hours blacked out! Cradock came in smiling.

"Why are you sedating me so heavily?" I whispered.

"It's on your chart, it's to relax you."

"I'm hungry."

"I'm sorry, Wiles, but you missed the evening meal."

Cradock then kicked my leg. I grimaced.

"Just checking your reflex actions," he smirked.

He started adjusting the hoist.

"It's time to put you to bed."

"But it's only 9PM!"

He got me into the sling and hoisted me onto the bed. The next thing I knew, Cradock injected me again. Before I blacked out, he said:

"See you in the morning." He walked out of the room.

***

In the morning, I woke up with a splitting headache.

"How are we today, Wiles?" said Cradock putting me in the wheelchair.

"I've got a headache with tingling sensations in my body."

"Those symptoms are due to the electrical storms in your brain, Wiles," Cradock was smiling, "That's why I'm going to give you an electric shock treatment today."

"What! I don't need electric shock treatment."

"In my opinion you do and I'm the professional."

"You're torturing me!"

I struggled to get out of the chair but Cradock pushed me back and cuffed my hands to the arms of the wheelchair. Then he gave me an injection of something.

"This will relax you during the treatment," said Cradock, "I'll make your bed while the jab is taking hold."

I sat in the wheelchair getting dizzier by the minute. I looked at Cradock tiding my bed with blurred vision. I felt a numbness, I was paralyzed in the chair, but I was aware of everything going on, but I couldn't speak! I started drooling. Cradock wiped my mouth and off we went to the electric therapy room.

Cradock released the cuffs and lifted me onto a table. He strapped my arms and legs. Then he hooked me up to a machine that took my vital signs. I could barely see the squiggly lines on the monitor. I couldn't speak or move, it was like being in a nightmare.

"I hope you are comfortable, Wiles," said my wicked carer.

Cradock placed an airway tube in my mouth to aid my breathing, he said. He also stuck a rubber bit in my mouth to clamp down on. He put electrodes on the sides of my head on the temple areas. He turned on the electricity for a couple of seconds. My whole body seemed to stiffen up. Then he gave me another jolt of electricity, now my whole body was twitching violently!

I was scared to death by this time. The electrodes were tight, they felt like they were denting my skull. Then another jolt of electricity shook me to the core. This was like mediaeval torture!

I felt hot than cold, the shaking wouldn't stop. Cradock was smiling through the entire thirty minute procedure. I was exhausted when Cradock got me back to my room and lifted me onto my bed and covered me.

"You will get your body movement and speech back in about thirty minutes. I'll be back to see how you are."

He left me staring at the ceiling. My body was still having tremors and then I lost consciousness

***

When I woke up, every muscle in my body pained me. I felt like a truck ran over me. I looked around the room, I felt confused and fuzzy headed. I started wringing my hands and playing with the buttons on my pajamas. Then Cradock came in.

"You're awake, Wiles, how do you feel?"

"Terrible."

"Well, lets hope we got rid of those "storms" in your brain."

Cradock stared at me while he checked my pulse.

"Lets see how you look. The pupils of your eyes are larger than normal and your skin is flushed. You keep clenching your teeth. I would stop that or you might bite your tongue."

Cradock was trying to act professional, like he really cared about me.

"You will probably have some memory loss and bouts of confusion for a day or so, but hopefully things will return to normal," he said smiling, showing his white teeth.

All of a sudden I felt a sickly urge.

"Take me to the toilet fast."

Cradock lifted me out of bed and placed me on the toilet just in time. This was the after effect of the shock treatment. The next thing I knew I was back in bed. I felt so weak I couldn't move. I lost consciousness.

***

The days went by in a succession of "torture", my word. Cradock called it, "keeping to the schedule". One day he put me to bed at 3PM and I never saw him again until the next morning. Needless to say, my incontinence pad was soaked and leaking! Everyday I was groggy and I knew Cradock was overdosing me with drugs. I also had migraines during the day, but I wasn't going to tell the wicked one, for fear of more electro therapy!

As the days passed I was getting more and more depressed. Cradock started giving me antidepressants along with the sedative jab. I started to think about suicide. I tried to stop those thoughts but I couldn't. I had a crippling fear of Cradock.

One day he wheeled me into the treatment room.

"I'm going to check your vitals and take a blood sample."

He couldn't find a vein right away and I ended up with a huge black and blue mark. After that exercise I was very tired, so Cradock put me to bed. I fell asleep right away. When I woke I was in the shower chair.

"You're going to have a shower, Wiles, " he said, turning on the cold water.

"Aaaah! Get me out of here, it's freezing," I screamed.

Cradock has shut the heavy door, no one could hear me and I passed out for a minute. When I came to, the torturer was wheeling me out of the shower. He dried me off but I was shivering and my teeth were chattering. My body was covered with goose-bumps and I was blue with cold!

Sometimes, Cradock wouldn't bother me too much. Like the day he let me alone with my coloring book.

"So, it's true that the patients sit around and color for therapy?"

"Yes it's true," said Cradock walking away and leaving me alone for four hours.

It was so relaxing in the day room coloring without Cradock breathing down my neck. There is something very therapeutic about coloring. Maybe, it took me back to my childhood and maybe, the back and forth movement of the crayon was quieting.

Jehovah wasn't coloring, he was busy listening to voices.

"I know the voices aren't real," he said, "But I can't stop hearing them!"

He looked spaced out, I hoped he wouldn't fly into a rage and ruin my coloring time.

Life Story Terror

***

The next day, Cradock left me in bed past breakfast. That was okay by me because my legs were hurting and I couldn't move them.

"Are you going to get me up today?" I wondered what torture he had up his sleeve today.

"You need to rest today. I think it's warm in here, I'll turn the heat down for a while."

It didn't take long for the room to get cold. I was freezing! Two hours later Cradock came back.

"Oh, sorry Wiles, I forgot the heat was off."

He came over and plumped up my pillows and smiled down at me.

"I think I'll give you a sponge wash now."

He started undressing me, I struggled but Cradock persevered and I ended up naked as a jaybird on a rubber sheet.

He laughed and said:

"You're as helpless as a baby. Look at you, you're an old wrinkled hulk."

"You're a brute, Cradock," I stammered, "My body might be old and wrinkled but every wrinkled up body has a human being inside with feelings. I deserve to be treated with kindness and respect."

He roared with laughter and continued with the sponge bath. And he was very rough with the sponge. When he put me to bed that night, my skin was raw and sore. I complained about my treatment, but the other nurses said I was imagining things and exaggerating. So I stopped complaining.

***

About a week later, Cradock left me in my room without injecting me with sedatives. I started to think how I could get out of this continual torture. I looked around the room and my gaze stopped on the electric hoist, which Cradock used every night to put me into bed. The sling, which was attached to the hoist, had four straps with loops. Maybe, just maybe, I could release myself from this bondage. I was losing weight because Cradock was only giving me one meal a day. He was killing me slowly with drugs. How long could I endure this slow torture?

***

That night at 8:30PM…
    "Well, Wiles, it's bedtime."
    I didn't realize I had a smile on my face.
    "What are you smiling about?" said Cradock, slapping me hard across my mouth. It stung but it didn't bleed.
    I had to end this 130 odd year revenge vendetta of the Cradock family. He had his back turned to me, getting the hoist ready. I reach for my bedside table lamp, which had a heavy base.
    "What are you up to?" He said, turning to me.
    I released the lamp.

"Nothing," I mumbled.

He gave me a menacing look.

"I think I'll give you your nighttime injection. There is enough sedative in here to put you away for good!"

"No, no!" I started to squirm in my wheelchair. But he jabbed me quickly. I felt the sedative juice going into me. My life flashed before my eyes as the injection was coursing through my veins. There were images racing through my mind.

I remembered seeing my grandfather at the port of entry in America. I also saw my grandmother on the steamship to America. I saw Janos Kovac burning my grandparent's house. I remembered the day I was at the tavern where my parents met. Then all the horrors of the Cradock's vendetta passed through my brain. The faces of the four Cradock men and Janos Kovac were speeding past. They all were laughing loudly. It was shocking.

Please stop this nightmare! I was sweating profusely. I was dying and I was having a life review, a self-reflection. I reviewed all three families, Wiles, Mickons, and Cradocks. I remembered all my good times with Charlie, my loyal King Charles spaniel.

I've heard of these phenomenon in which a person rapidly sees the totality of their lives. In the dying process the brain goes into hyper speed. Chemical changes in the brain light up my conscious memory. I'm aware of every single memory I've ever had. It is an amazing but frightening experience, because you never have access to every detail of your life, except now!

***

Then, a bright flash of light, and I was back in my white room. I had to move fast now, to beat the effect of the drug. I grabbed the lamp and struck Cradock hard on his head. He crumpled to the floor. I struggled over to him, and with all my remaining strength, I wound one end of the sling around his neck. He had already attached the other end to the sling bar. I pressed the "UP" button and the lift raised Cradock's body off the floor.

There he was, hanging by his neck, a small amount of blood trickling from his head wound onto his white coat! He would be dead in a minute or two. My suffering was over. The terror of the revenge vendetta was over.

Suddenly, I felt a sharp pain in my chest and I could feel myself blacking out. The last thing I saw was Charlie's picture on my dresser!

TIMELINE 2016

THE END

Printed in Great Britain
by Amazon